FROM OUR FIRST

Special Edition

CARRIE ANN RYAN

FROM OUR FIRST

A PROMISE ME NOVEL

By

Carrie Ann Ryan

FROM OUR FIRST

A Promise Me Novel

By: Carrie Ann Ryan

ISBN: 978-1-63695-292-5

Cover by Murphy Rae

Praise for Carrie Ann Ryan

“Count on Carrie Ann Ryan for emotional, sexy, character driven stories that capture your heart!” – Carly Phillips, NY Times bestselling author

“Carrie Ann Ryan’s romances are my newest addiction! The emotion in her books captures me from the very beginning. The hope and healing hold me close until the end. These love stories will simply sweep you away.” ~ NYT Bestselling Author Deveny Perry

"Carrie Ann Ryan writes the perfect balance of sweet and heat ensuring every story feeds the soul." - Audrey Carlan, #1 New York Times Bestselling Author

“Carrie Ann Ryan never fails to draw readers in with passion, raw sensuality, and characters that pop off the page. Any book by Carrie Ann is an absolute treat.” – New York Times Bestselling Author J. Kenner

“Carrie Ann Ryan knows how to pull your heart-strings and make your pulse pound! Her wonderful Redwood Pack series will draw you in and keep you reading long into the night. I can’t wait to see what comes next with the new generation, the Talons. Keep them coming, Carrie Ann!” –Lara Adrian, New York Times bestselling author of CRAVE THE NIGHT

"With snarky humor, sizzling love scenes, and brilliant, imaginative worldbuilding, The Dante's Circle series reads as if Carrie Ann Ryan peeked at my personal wish list!" – NYT Bestselling Author, Larissa Ione

"Carrie Ann Ryan writes sexy shifters in a world full of passionate happily-ever-afters." – *New York Times* Bestselling Author Vivian Arend

"Carrie Ann's books are sexy with characters you can't help but love from page one. They are heat and heart blended to perfection." *New York Times* Bestselling Author Jayne Rylon

Carrie Ann Ryan's books are wickedly funny and deliciously hot, with plenty of twists to keep you guessing. They'll keep you up all night!" USA Today Bestselling Author Cari Quinn

"Once again, Carrie Ann Ryan knocks the Dante's Circle series out of the park. The queen of hot, sexy, enthralling paranormal romance, Carrie Ann is an author not to miss!" *New York Times* bestselling Author Marie Harte

To Chelle.

Never change.

FROM OUR FIRST

New York Times and USA Today bestselling author Carrie Ann Ryan concludes her steamy contemporary stand-alone series with a secret that no one saw coming.

Nate Brady and Myra West have been keeping a secret, though not just from their group—also from each other. Getting married when they were barely adults wasn't in the cards when they made their plans for their future. Divorcing one another amidst pain and heartbreak wasn't either.

Years have passed, wounds have scabbed over and scarred, but their anger remains.

If the two can open themselves to the impossible, they might be able to take that second chance. Only they'll also have to fight their fears, the lies between them, and the desire they thought long gone.

Except they aren't alone in their secrets, and if they aren't careful, they may just be taking them to their graves.

Prologue

Myra

The moment I met Nathan, I knew I wanted to spend the rest of my life without him. Only it hadn't worked out the way I'd wanted to.

Nothing had worked out the way I'd wanted it to.

My heels echoed on the hardwood as I made my way toward where I'd seen the person in question slink off. For a man usually the face of the party, I was surprised that he wasn't smiling with the others and acting as if he weren't a giant, selfish asshole with more barbs than heart.

I held back a sigh, knowing those thoughts were only part of the reason I needed to find him.

We couldn't go on living this way.

I missed sleep. I missed my perfectly ordered life where I could pretend that the world wasn't horrible, and I hadn't shattered into a thousand pieces thanks to a calm cruelty that had shocked me to my very core.

And that meant I had to work with the man who haunted my days and threatened the peace of my nights.

I passed the others that I knew were related to Nate through marriage somehow and nodded, trying to smile with my eyes since my clenched jaw wouldn't allow anything else.

They wouldn't see the ice queen.

Good.

I needed Nate to see that queen, though.

She could wrap herself in armor. Could protect herself.

I needed to be that other me.

I turned the corner and spotted him in the library. He rubbed his temple before turning to me. A small part of me wanted to reach out and see if I could do something for his pain.

But I wasn't that girl anymore.

And he'd never been that boy.

I let the ice queen reign.

"We need to talk."

Nate looked up at me, and I raised a brow, so tired of the clutch in my belly at the sight of him. "Do we?"

"You know why, Nathan."

"I honestly don't."

He lied. He had to. And I hated him for it. I loathed how he made me feel. The way he'd once been my everything. I hated him more with each passing day.

And what was worse, I despised the idea that he made me hate myself.

"Yes, we do, *husband*."

Nate flinched and looked past me as if to see if anyone were near. What would he do if someone overheard? If they knew the truth of my greatest mistake? "Don't fucking call me that."

I raised my chin, narrowing my eyes at the man who'd broken me. "Fine. *Ex-husband*. Whatever title you want to use. But we're going to talk."

Chapter 1

Myra

"That's crap. Complete and utter crap." I set down my paintbrush and looked at the canvas in front of me, cursing out loud. "Complete shit."

There was nobody in my studio so I could curse, shout, and act as unladylike as I wanted.

However, I still looked over my shoulder as if afraid my mother would show up out of the blue just to see what I was doing. I had a feeling she knew the precise moment I cursed—when I had a drink…or three.

She probably also knew every time that I had sex,

not that that was very often. Or any time in recent memory.

I frowned and looked down at my fingers, trying to do the math. No, I wouldn't think about that. I might be dusty and a little like a forgotten cavern, but I was still a woman. Sexy. And I was running late. Hence the cursing.

My ringer had gone off on my phone, the final alarm that told me that I absolutely had to be out the door in ten minutes if I had any chance of making my coffee date at the Boulder Bean.

I looked at my canvas, at the portrait of colors before me, and shook my head.

I wasn't in it. I couldn't feel the piece.

Not that it mattered. I still had time to work on my next project. My art made me a nice living, yet I knew it was my investments and my trust fund that had gotten me where I was now.

And my mother never let me forget that.

I shook my head at the thought of her. Twice in one meltdown. I needed to get my mother out of my head.

And I honestly did not want to go to the Boulder Bean. My best friends would be there, sure, but I knew what they were waiting for. Me. And it was all my fault. I was Icarus, had flown far too close to the sun. I was the reason for my personal downfall. I had pushed the others far too hard in our pact, and now it was my turn.

Of course, I hadn't thought we'd get this far. I'd figured once the straws were drawn, we wouldn't actually go through with the rest of the deal. I didn't think I would be forced on a blind date with a stranger when I wasn't even sure what I wanted in the first place. The gods of fate had blessed me with being fourth in line for this ridiculous pact of ours, but somehow, the farce had become truth.

And now, it was my turn.

I wasn't going. I could stay home and hide from the world—something I was getting far too good at these days.

I cleaned up my brushes and the rest of my area before I washed my hands and took off my painting smock. I still wore a decent outfit underneath, and because I hadn't been painting very well, I hadn't gotten a single spot on me. That probably meant I'd only been staring at the canvas and its few brush strokes and doing my best to forget why I was so stressed out.

I did not want to go on a blind date.

I couldn't.

If I were to go, that meant I would need to be across from somebody at a table, eating a meal. I would have to get to know them. I would need to speak to the person in front of me and tell them my fears and my likes and dislikes.

I felt as if I didn't know what those were. Or maybe I didn't know what I *should* like to please others. And since that wasn't in my wheelhouse, I was floundering. I knew what I liked. I was very particular. Everybody thought Paris was the careful planner, but they were wrong. I was the one firm in my decisions and steadfast in my needs.

I had changed the course of my life when my heart was shattered into a million pieces.

I was not going to think about that, though. I would push *him* from my mind.

No, not him. He did not exist.

I wasn't going to think about him at all.

Damn it, now I was thinking about him. Of his hazel eyes and dark hair. I would *not* think about that chiseled jaw. Or the fact that he had filled out since we first met. No, I would not think about that. Because if I did, I might as well just shove that paint scraper right into my eye and call it a day.

My phone buzzed, and I looked down at it.

Of course, it wasn't a text. *Of course*, my friend would call so I had to be careful with my voice and my answers. It wouldn't matter in the end anyway, because she'd be able to read me regardless.

"Hello there, Paris. How are you today?" I asked, putting on my best voice.

"I'm probably doing much better than you are, Ms. Myra."

"Why, whatever do you mean?"

"Do not take that lady of the manor tone with me. You might be a rich girl, but I have the power here."

I inwardly cringed at that because I didn't like the fact that she was right. She did have all the power, and I *was* a little rich girl.

I was the friend with the trust fund, the pearls around her neck when she turned ten who had gone off to boarding school and then been offered entrance into every single Ivy League college I wanted to attend.

My one act of rebellion had turned into a horrendous mistake for everybody involved and was a complete breach of trust.

I was everything Paris thought I was—and the worst version of it.

"Why am I like this?" I asked myself, not realizing that I had said the words out loud until Paris snorted over the phone.

"You're like this because you're scared. Remember, I have the power." Paris laughed. "I'm sure you look wonderful as always. Now, slip your feet out of your work shoes and into those sexy yet casual heels you wear whenever you're in the coffee shop, grab your purse, and get your ass over here. It is your turn, and we are not going to let you get out of this."

I winced, trying to think of a way out of this reality. "I think after everything that's happened with our crew, our sisterhood, maybe it's time to take a step back and reaffirm what we have."

"No, no. Save all of your backpedaling for when you're in front of us. You know I don't care."

"Paris," I said, shocked and yet not even a little bit surprised.

"Don't *Paris* me. You pushed me into this pact, and I went on some seriously horrendous dates."

"But you got the love of your life out of the deal, so it worked out." I shut my mouth even as the words fell from my lips. Why had I said that? Maybe because I always had to be right. Because I had to prove to Paris that pushing her into the pact had been good for her.

And now it was going to bite me on the ass.

Damn it.

"We're not even going to dignify that with a response, are we? Especially considering you helped my case and all. You're going to get your ass over here, and we're going to figure out what we need to do with you, Ms. Myra, darling."

"Paris."

"Nope. Get dressed, or we will come to you. We will circle you like vultures. Happy and in love vultures, waiting for you to take the next step. You pushed us into this, Myra. And now it's your turn."

Paris let out a cackle and then hung up the phone.

I just blinked down at the black screen and shook my head.

"Overdramatic much?" I asked.

A text popped up on the screen.

Paris: *Yes, that was overdramatic, but I've been practicing my evil witch laugh, and I think I have it down. Now, get your ass over here. Immediately. Or I'm going to send a certain someone over there to pick you up, and it's not going to be one of us girls.*

I froze. I knew exactly who she'd send over here. And it wouldn't be one of the men my best friends had fallen in love with. It wouldn't be another friend or a casual coworker.

No, it would be the one person that I could not be in the same room with. Despite our tentative truce, I knew Paris would get what she wanted.

She'd get under my skin, ruffle my feathers, and do all of the other metaphors out there to piss me the fuck off.

I had to do this. I could do this. A couple of dates, a few cute and casual glasses of wine with some very handsome men—hopefully, ones that didn't talk about their mothers all the time, and didn't have a *Dexter* basement full of tarps and easily accessible chainsaws.

I shivered at that thought and had to tell myself once again not to have that image. I'd only made it three episodes into the series before I had to stop watching it because of the nightmares. Now, they would all come back.

Maybe I could watch a marathon of *Dexter* instead of going out and dating. Yes, that sounded like a much better idea.

Paris: *I know you're spiraling right now, and I don't know where you're going in that mind of yours, but I'm sure it's scary and probably has an ax murderer in it.*

I was a little worried about how well Paris knew me at this point. If I was at all attracted to her, maybe I should've dated her.

Of course, Paris was happy and in love with Prior. And, really, I should get over myself. But, seriously. It was a little spooky.

Me: *Okay, I will change into my shoes and come over. But no shenanigans.*

Paris: *Honey, you're about to get all the shenanigans. You earned it.*

I sighed, cursing at myself. This whole situation was my fault. I did deserve this. All of it. I just really hated that I had no control.

OUR FRIEND DAKOTA owned the Boulder Bean, a cute little coffee shop and bakery right in the heart of Boulder. I loved this area. Even though it wasn't my hometown, I had made it my home.

The city was filled with every type of person you could possibly imagine.

The business executive on his way to a meeting. Of course, that guy probably had a mountain home or liked to snowboard or wasn't exactly the New York or LA kind of guy I was used to in my past.

There was also the mom with her five kids, looking frazzled but excited because they were outside in the fresh air, the beautiful mountains the perfect backdrop for any occasion.

Then there were the crunchy granola hipsters, the ones that kept Boulder weird.

The college students. The ones either half-baked, fully baked, or completely exhausted because I had a feeling it was midterm season given what my friend Hazel had said. She taught at one of the main universities in the city. Though the huge university was the University of Colorado, Boulder University was up-and-coming.

All of those people plus many more made Boulder unique, and all the weird that it wanted to be. It was completely different from what I had grown up with, and precisely what I needed. I might've tried to go to college for a bit in Denver, but that hadn't worked out. And I didn't want to think about it. I couldn't.

Once again, I pushed that out of my mind and told myself that I would talk about it with my therapist. The next time I went. If that ever happened.

I looked up at the small coffee shop and smiled. The place was busy, Dakota's steady stream of customers loyal and increasing by the day. She was doing amazingly, and I was so proud of her.

She had been through hell and back more than once in her life, and now she and her son and Macon were making things right. They were a family. And they were doing wonderfully.

I ignored the little clutch in my belly at that. It wasn't that I wasn't happy for her. I was beyond happy. But there was jealousy there, too. And there shouldn't be. I shouldn't be envious of an idea that wouldn't change my outcome.

And I hated that I knew that. I wanted the idea of that family. The idea that I could have one. I wanted that. I desired that happiness. I had tried for it once, but I had been wrong. So, yes, I was jealous of my friends. And I hated that. But I knew if I went for it, if I walked in there, I still wouldn't have what they did.

Because I would never have *him*.

"Suck it up, Myra," I said and walked through the

doors, a little out of breath. "Hello there, girls," I added, making my way to our usual booth.

Hazel sat there, her tablet in her hand as she worked through something. Work or planning her wedding, I wasn't sure. She was starting to get that bridal fever, and I kind of loved it.

She and Cross were made for each other, even though they'd almost lost everything to get where they were. Much like everybody else at this table had. Somehow, the courtships brought about through this pact system of ours had created a craziness that I still couldn't explain.

But it had worked out for them.

I didn't think there was enough fate and magic pixie dust left in the universe to make it work for me, though.

"There you are," Paris said, setting her enormous paper planner down beside her. The thing seemed to increase in size every time I looked at it, and I couldn't help but hold back a smile.

"I promised I'd be here. Hello, Paris. And Paris's planner."

"Are you making fun of my planner?" Paris asked in her most haughty tone.

"Maybe." I took a seat across the booth from her.

My friend narrowed her eyes at me. "Beware, I will

write down in my planner that I will have to smite you if you continue to do so."

Hazel took a sip of her drink and snorted some foam. "Smite?" she asked, and I shook my head, doing my best not to let my lips twitch.

"Is it smote? Or smoted?" I asked, playing along to annoy Paris.

"Please stop trying to make up words when you don't understand." Paris scrunched her nose.

"You just threatened to smite me, so I'm not exactly sure you have a leg to stand on," I said.

"Speaking of promises, I'm glad you came." Dakota set an herbal tea in front of me. It smelled lovely and was already made perfectly with a dash of honey and a dollop of cream.

"Oh, thank you." I brought it to my nose to inhale its scent. "It smells divine."

Paris sighed. "If you're done making love to your tea, let's talk about that promise you made. A pact, indeed."

I narrowed my eyes into slits as I stared at Paris and casually took a sip of my drink. It was the perfect temperature.

Dakota was a genius.

"Scooch," Dakota said, and I sighed, setting down my cup and sliding across the booth.

"Shouldn't you be working?" I asked.

"I have been, but I'm not allowed to be on my leg for too many hours a day or Macon starts growling."

I winced, having been so entirely focused on myself that I had forgotten that Dakota had been injured. "I'm so sorry. Are you okay? What can I do? Do I need to get you coffee?"

Dakota laughed, shaking her head. "No, I got myself some earlier. And don't worry, I'm fine. This is my allotted break time, though. And it is time for the final straw."

Hazel clapped her hands in front of her. "Yes. Just wait until you see the list I have for you."

"Me, too!" Paris said, clapping her hands together.

"You have lists?" I asked, wondering why I felt nauseous and excited at the same time.

I had thought maybe they'd try to put me together with Nate. It only made sense. Everybody could tell something was going on between us. The girls liked to joke that it may sound like hate, but it had to be sexual attraction.

I was not sexually attracted to Nathan Brady.

There.

And since we were all in the same group, four men and four women, and with three couples already paired up, it would only make sense for me to be with Nate.

But it *didn't* make sense. At all. I was not going to be with Nathan Brady.

And I had to stop saying his name like that, or every memory I had of him would come back to me, and I would likely throw up.

"I have a list, too." Dakota smiled

"I'm really worried about this. I thought we exhausted our lists with Paris. There were a lot of men on that list," I said dryly.

Paris discreetly flipped me off. "They were all duds, and the guy we set Hazel up with originally is back with his wife. However, we have been waiting for this. You are the perfect person for the men we couldn't be with," Paris added and blinked as her words caught up with her.

I sighed. "Thanks for that. All of your rejects are for me."

"No, not rejects. Simply not perfect matches. I do believe we can find your perfect match," Hazel corrected.

I'd thought I already found it.

I ignored that thought once again. What was wrong with me? I had gone years without thinking of Nate like this. Apparently, having him in my life daily and trying to talk to one another and not fight all the time just put him on the periphery more.

I couldn't ignore him. I couldn't overlook the memories.

I couldn't forget that I knew what he felt like

hovering over me as he gently kissed me, taking me to sensual places I'd never been before.

But then the memories overlapped one another. The idea that I knew what he looked like when he lost all faith. Or the betrayal that slid over a person when they realized that the one they thought they loved more than anything didn't trust them.

No, I wasn't going to think about that.

"So, what you're saying is that I have a lot of men to choose from?" I asked. Yes, I needed to do this. Because the more I thought about Nate, the worse it would be for everybody. Nate and I needed to learn to be friends. We hadn't exactly been that before, and somehow, we needed to figure it out now.

Because I could not be Nate's.

And he certainly wasn't mine.

I had lost that hope long ago, given up on that promise. I would make a new one. To anyone that I could. Anyone but Nate.

"Okay, girls, sign me up," I blurted.

They all stared at me, blinking.

"Really?" Paris asked. She let out an *oof* as Hazel elbowed her.

"What Paris means is that it took you a lot to get here, and now you're about to lean into it. You aren't going to forget to show up for these dates, right? Because that would be rude. And you are not rude."

Hazel paused. "Okay, you can be rude sometimes, but not to strangers." She paused again. "Okay, what I mean is—"

I cut her off, holding up my hand. "No, no. I think I know where you're going with this, and the more you keep digging that hole, the harder it is for me to remain your friend."

"Sorry," she mumbled.

"No, I understand. I'm the icy bitch queen. It gets me where I need to be. However, we talked about promises. And I'm not going back on that."

Plus, I needed a future—an idea of a promise that wasn't with Nate. So, I would do this. I was going on some dates and maybe I'd find *the one*. Or perhaps just get Nate out of my mind.

"Okay, so we have a list," Dakota said.

"I might not be looking for forever," I began and cut the others off before they could say anything. "You all got lucky. I understand that forever might not be for everyone. However, I do agree to this, so I'm in. Let the dating begin."

And, once again, I ignored the slight twinge in my heart.

I had once thought I'd found my happily ever after, but it wasn't meant to be.

I had learned the hard way, and that was fine.

Because now I had a second chance. Maybe not at true happiness, but at least at contentment.

As I looked around at my friends, pure joy and satisfaction radiating off them, I knew I needed to find *something*. Because I had been alone for long enough.

And I was afraid if I didn't take this chance, I would be forever.

Chapter 2

Nate

"You want me to what?" I asked, staring at my brother.

"I want you to go on a date," Prior said, steepling his hands in front of himself.

"You aren't Professor X. You don't need to give me that look."

Prior looked down at his hands and smirked. "I don't know, I think Magneto does this more than Professor X. Or maybe that's because Ian McKellen does it more than Patrick Stewart."

"That's true, we could watch the movies and decide. Of course, we may need to watch the cartoon from the nineties as well, to make sure. And I think I still have a few of my old comics. If not, we can go look them up. Did you know that they have digital comics now? And they work cool where they slide right across the page instead of like a normal book. It sort of goes from frame to frame."

My brother's eyes brightened. "Yes, that would be—wait... Did you just get me distracted that quickly with an X-Men reference?" Prior asked, and I did my best not to smile.

"I have no idea what you're talking about. This is legitimate research."

He shook his head. "Either way, we both agree that the third movie of each trilogy is the worst. It is the curse of *X3*."

I grimaced. "It is. So maybe we should skip those and move on to the next set and pretend *X3* never existed."

"That is what we've always decided. And stop distracting me. Tonight, you need to go on a date."

I shook my head. "No, that's the pact sisters. The girls do blind dates."

"Yes, and I think it ended up quite nicely so far," Prior said, smiling dreamily.

If I didn't get Prior out of here soon, he would

start talking about Paris and get even more blissful, and I'd have to deal with the sickly sweetness of it all.

I didn't begrudge my brother's happiness. Hell, I was one of the first in our family to like the guy that our little sister, Arden, married. Arden was my twin, but she was so much smaller and frailer, that I thought of her as the baby.

Every single one of my siblings was happy and either married or engaged. They were already talking about adoptions and pregnancies, and Macon even had a son with Dakota since the two were already working on the paperwork to make Joshua a Brady legally.

Everybody was taking steps into their futures, but I was at a stalemate. I was fine with that, though. I didn't need a future of happiness and marriage and babies. That was simply what society told the world a person needed.

"Why are you sitting there staring into space?" Prior asked.

"I was just thinking about societal norms. I don't need to conform. We are in a new age where we can follow whatever paths we want to."

"Of course. But first, you're going to follow the pact rules." Prior gave a tight nod.

I frowned. "I thought Cross and Macon were the bossy ones. Where do you get off?" At Prior's leer, I gave a full-body shudder. "Let me rephrase that."

"I'm not going to talk about that right now. Especially since we've already discussed Paris today."

I made a gagging sound. "Thank you. I hate this. I need to go burn this room so I never have to think about it again."

"This is your house. You don't need to burn it. Maybe burn some sage or throw some salt in the corners. You're fine." Prior grinned. "However, as I was saying, you can go and do whatever societal norms you want. *After* you do this."

"I'm not going on another date. I'm fine. I went on a date like three weeks ago."

"You attended a business dinner with a couple of your clients who are married to each other and you were the third wheel. Unless you're entering into a triad situation. If that's what you truly decide, then we support you. But you're going on a date tonight."

"What if I had plans?" I asked.

"You're Nate. If you had plans, it would have been with one of us, and we already talked. You don't have plans."

"I have friends other than you," I said, affronted.

"Whatever you say. I believe you. Especially with you leaving the house all the time since you now work from home."

I clenched my jaw, and Prior had the grace to wince. "Fuck. That's not what I meant. I know that you love your current job, and you left your old one for medical reasons. I wasn't insinuating anything. Shit. I'm sorry. Let's start over."

"I know you didn't mean anything by it. I don't need to be an EMT anymore. I do just fine as a copywriter. It's a completely different path than I thought I would be on, but…here we are. I like my life. I have a steady job. I'm saving for retirement. I need to pay for my medical insurance, but that's neither here nor there."

"That's always here, but I digress," Prior began. "It's time for you to find somebody. You don't need to fall in love on the first date, just get out of the house."

"Why is it that happy couples want to set up all of their single friends?"

My brother scowled. "You helped push Macon in the right direction, why are you hesitating now?"

"I pushed Macon because he was madly in love with Dakota and refused to see it."

Prior shook his head. "Okay, that's a good reason. However, you saw a good outcome with that. Why don't you think you can have a good one?"

Because I already had one.

I wasn't going down that path. I'd done it once

before, and I had been betrayed in the end. I wouldn't allow myself to get stuck in that cycle again.

"I don't want to do this."

"Okay, just once."

I narrowed my eyes at Prior. "How does *just once* fit with me not doing it at all?" I asked.

"Because if you do it once, then the family will move on to something else and forget that we put you in this situation."

"Are you now playing good cop/bad cop with the Bradys? Because that was a bizarre episode."

"Stop making *Brady Bunch* jokes." Prior's eyes twinkled.

I snorted. "I'm just saying. And with our last name, they come out of nowhere."

"That is true. Thank God we're older now. Because when we were kids? That was ridiculous."

"Mostly with the parents," I said, reminiscing before we burst out laughing.

"Seriously. Just try it out. It's only dinner and drinks. And if it sucks, you can go home. But at least you can say you tried."

"What if I don't want to?"

"What if I dare you?" Prior asked, smug satisfaction in his gaze.

. . .

AND THAT WAS how I found myself standing at a host stand, my hair clean and pushed back from my face, ready for a blind date.

I could have said no to many things. But a dare when it came to my pesky and annoying bigger brother? No, I couldn't back down.

Prior had been one second away from clucking like a chicken. So now here I was, caught in the middle because I was an idiot.

I moved up to the hostess stand and smiled. "Hi. I'm here for Smith, party of two."

"Ah, Smith," the woman said, a wicked gleam in her eyes.

I didn't know if that boded well for me. Maybe she knew it was an alias. Apparently, the brothers wanted to make sure that it was a completely blind date. So, here I was, unable to use my name or know the last name of the person I was supposed to meet.

"Your party is already here. I will take you to your table now."

"Thank you."

"I sure hope you have a wonderful time, Mr. Smith."

I nearly tripped over my feet at her tone. "Did you have a photo of me so you knew I was the right Smith or something?"

The hostess beamed. "Yes. I was also told that if

you try to run, I'm supposed to make clucking sounds. I refuse. However, I do have a recording of who I believe are your brothers making those chicken sounds."

"Why would I run from my date?" I asked, but I didn't need her to answer. I didn't need the hostess to say anything because I knew what had happened.

Myra sat at the table, looking regal and sexy as fuck in a tight black dress that showed off her curves with the tiniest bit of cleavage that begged me to look.

I wasn't going to look.

Simply because I knew what she looked like naked when we were younger, didn't mean I knew what she looked like under her clothes now. And I wasn't going to imagine it either. She had filled out a bit more and looked even sexier than she had when we were together, but that didn't mean I needed to focus on it.

Her honey-blond hair had been curled back from her face, the tips brushing her shoulders. She looked gorgeous, sweet. And I knew that once she looked up, I would see those blue eyes. And I would fall.

I would hate myself.

"Here you go, Mr. Smith." The hostess walked away as Myra's gaze shot up. Her mouth dropped in surprise, and I saw…mortification in her eyes.

"You," she stuttered.

I didn't want to make a scene, but I had no idea

what I was supposed to do. If I ran, there would be fucking clucking noises. I had a feeling that my brothers had either bribed the hostess well, or the woman was somehow friends with our friends. I wasn't sure. But, Jesus Christ. I *couldn't* run now.

Though if I sat down, I wouldn't be doing so in front of the woman who was friends with my friends. No, I would be sitting down with my ex-wife, our past between us like a third person in our party.

However, I didn't have a way out of this, and I wasn't sure I could outrun the chickens, let alone my past. No, there was no turning back. And, honestly, I didn't think there ever had been—not since I saw Myra across the room after so many years that first time.

So, I took a deep breath and sat down across from her, ignoring how her hand tightened around her phone. "Hello, Myra."

"Did you set this up?" she asked, her voice a hiss.

"No, your friends and my family did. Because they have a cruel sense of humor."

She flinched. Tonight wasn't what I had expected, and yet, there was no going back.

"They told me they had lists of dozens of names for me to go through for this pact so I could find my date and happiness. But, apparently, you were first on the list. Now I'm a little worried to see who's next."

My head hurt, and I couldn't reconcile my lack of

control over anything. Which was probably why I sounded like an asshole when I next opened my mouth. "Apparently, I *am* your list, baby."

"Don't call me *baby*," she snapped before closing her eyes and letting out a breath. "We need to stop doing this. We told ourselves that we would stop doing this."

My hand fisted on the table, and I nodded, forcing myself to relax. "You're right. We may hate each other, but we have to be friends."

Once again, she flinched, but it was the truth. We did hate each other. We had thrown the words at each other before. There was no taking them back. "How are we going to do this?"

"We did just fine when we were watching Joshua when Dakota lost all her babysitters."

Her lips went white under her gloss as she tightened them. "Because we had a common purpose—to keep him safe. But we still fought."

I nodded, frowning down at the menu. "True. But why do I feel like the animosity has only increased since?"

"Maybe because it has?" she asked and then sighed. "I hate this. I hate that I don't feel comfortable in my skin when you're around."

I frowned.

"Not like that," she corrected. "Because I feel like

I'm two steps behind, and we have so many secrets. Huge secrets, Nate. And we're keeping them from our friends and family."

"We are," I said, knowing where she was going with this.

"They don't know why this is so horrible for us. They don't realize that we shouldn't be together across from each other at a table. Alone."

I sighed. "Are you saying we should tell them?"

She played with the wine glass as the waiter came. She looked up and put on her best smile, though I knew it didn't reach her eyes.

"If the gentleman is ready to order, I am," she began.

"Sure, I can find something quick."

"I'll have the salmon, only be sure there's no shellfish."

"Of course, ma'am."

"I'll take the filet," I said, looking down at the side dishes. I recognized a few things, but I wasn't sure I had ever had them together. This wasn't a place where you picked your sides. It was up to the chef, so I went with it.

"How would you like your steak cooked?"

"Medium-rare?" I asked, and Myra gave a slight nod. I hated that I felt relieved at that.

Whenever we went out when we were younger,

especially when we went to the fancy places for an anniversary or something, she helped me order. After all, she had grown up in that world. I was good at ordering from Applebees, not so much for places like this. Every once in a while, I went out to similar places with people I occasionally worked with, but it wasn't the same since it was a work thing. And while I always liked my steak medium-rare, apparently, being in front of Myra meant I felt like I needed confirmation.

I hated that feeling. Like we were stuck in the past, yet somehow needed to be in the future.

It made no sense.

"We'll get that right out. Would you like bread?" the waiter asked.

"Sure." I didn't move my eyes from Myra.

"Their bread is delicious," Myra said, playing with her wine glass stem. "And back to if we should tell them… I don't know."

"If we do, maybe they'll stop trying to set us up," I countered.

"Perhaps. Or maybe the betrayal will be so great that they'll want nothing to do with us."

"Arden already knows."

Myra winced. "I know. But there was no keeping it from your twin. Especially not when she saw my ring."

"True. If we tell the rest of them, they're going to get upset with her, too."

"They damn well will not," Myra said. "We will take the blame for everything if and when we tell them. Arden does *not* get touched."

I tried to ignore the pride I felt at Myra stepping up and protecting my sister. I didn't know who I was to Myra, not anymore, and I didn't even know how I felt about her.

I hated what she did to me and who we were in the past, but I really didn't know this woman in front of me.

Maybe that was the problem.

"Your best friends are with my brothers. Every single one of them."

Myra nodded tightly. "There's no escaping that fact."

"I don't know how I can keep from being in my brothers' lives."

"I had to walk away from my life before. I'm not sure I can do it again," Myra said.

The truth of her words was too much of an echo of what had happened years ago. I didn't want to go down that path.

Not again.

"You're not my favorite person," I said, and she raised her glass in cheers.

"Ditto."

"But despite that," I continued, "I don't want to

take away what you have with them. I couldn't do that. Not even to you."

"You're really good with the barbs." She took a sip of her wine.

I took a sip of mine, letting it settle on my tongue before I swallowed. "I need to stop that. We aren't those people anymore, Myra."

She set her wine glass on the table and studied my face. "We aren't. And maybe it's time we remembered that."

"So you want to what? Clean the slate?" Because I wasn't sure I could do that. Not with the pain I remembered.

"I don't think there's ever going to be a fully clean slate between us. But maybe we can move past it, at least when we're forced into each other's circles. We've been doing that for how long now? Perhaps we need to continue and do it better."

"What does that mean?" I asked.

"I say we follow through with our truce. We talked about it at the cabin, but not enough."

I nodded. "I had a shitty headache that day, so I don't remember much of what we talked about."

She frowned. "A headache?"

"From the accident."

"Accident?" Myra asked.

It was so funny. The woman in front of me had

been with me during an important part of my life. *She* had *been* an important part of my life. But she didn't know what had happened in the years between then and now.

"I was an EMT. Our ambulance got T-boned, and I got a severe concussion. To the point where I will probably have symptoms for the rest of my life. Traumatic brain injury does that to a person."

Her eyes widened, and she reached out as if to grab my hand but pulled back at the last minute. I didn't know what I would have done if she had touched me. I never knew what to do when it came to Myra. And that was the problem.

Her face paled. "I didn't know. I always wondered why you weren't an EMT anymore, but I didn't want to ask."

"I love my job now. But no, I'm changed."

"And I'm not the girl that I was before either."

The silence the fell wasn't as awkward as it had been before, but it was still far too strained for my liking.

"So, what do we do?" I asked.

"I think we need to get over ourselves," she said and took a big gulp of wine. I did the same, reaching for bread as our waiter set it down.

She took a roll, carefully placed it on her plate, slice it open, used a slight corner of salted butter, and gently spread it over her bread. She was always so meticulous with her food as if she needed to be picture perfect. I knew it had come from her mother, but I tried my best not to notice what she did now. I didn't want to notice.

"So, we have a truce?" I asked into the silence.

"We don't have to be friends, Nate. I don't know if we can be friends."

I ignored the odd hurt that statement brought. Because her thoughts ran along the same lines as mine. I shouldn't feel any pain when it came to her and the feelings she evoked. "Okay. But we can be acquaintances. We can be part of the same circles. But we don't have to lob barbs at each other."

"We don't need to be cruel," she whispered, echoing my word from before.

"I don't think it's healthy for either of us to continue down a path where hatred burns between us."

She let out a breath and gave me a tight nod. "I agree. We'll figure out what we need to do in each situation, but I can promise that my first inclination will not be to sneer at you every time I see you."

I smiled at that. "And I will try not to be rude to you or get through doors before you."

"I always wondered if you did that on purpose," Myra said, smiling. This time, it reached her eyes, and I hated that I noticed.

"It was a little petty."

"We don't need to be friends. But we need to be kind," she said. "I think *kind* is a good word. Because our friends need that, they've been through so much. We can do that for them."

"I agree." I cleared my throat. "And since we're being kind, we're splitting the check."

"Oh, good, because you got the steak, and I got the salmon. Your meal is like twice as expensive as mine." Myra took a sip of her wine.

"That's fine with me."

"My next date will have to pay for my meal. For propriety's sake."

My stomach lurched at that, and I did my best not to frown. "I see. The girls are really going to work through their list?"

An odd look crossed her face, and then she smiled. "Of course. I'm the last part of the pact. It's their turn to find me the perfect date."

"And I'm not it," I said dryly, starting it off as a joke. But when her eyes filled with hurt for an instant, I immediately regretted the words.

Instead of saying something, not knowing *what* to say at all, I lifted my glass in cheers. "To you finding your perfect romance."

She clinked her glass to mine, her face carefully blank.

"And for it not to be you."

"Ouch."

"A final barb. And now, the truce is on."

I sipped my wine and hoped like hell I knew what that meant.

Chapter 3

Myra

"What do you mean it didn't work out?" Paris asked, and I pinched the bridge of my nose.

"It's what I said. I know you all had good intentions, but how about we go through the rest of the list and ignore anybody related to the Bradys?"

Hazel frowned, took out her notebook, and crossed off a few names.

That made me blink. "Why are you crossing people off?"

"You said nobody related to the Bradys."

"Are there cousins I wasn't aware of?" I asked, a little weirded out.

Hazel tilted her head as she studied her notes. "Yes, but that's beside the point. There are also non-Brady ones, and since Arden has a boatload of cousins now through Liam, some of whom aren't married, even though the rest of them seem to have all been paired off recently, I assume you don't want those either."

"How about we go with no one connected to your love lives at all?" I asked, doing my best to take deep breaths so I wouldn't stress out. It wasn't their fault that I wasn't handling this well. It wasn't their fault that I had no idea what I was doing or what I wanted.

The primary thing was that I needed to get Nate out of my mind. And to do that, I had to date someone else. I had already said that I would try so I wasn't alone. This was simply an extra incentive to do so. It didn't need to be the end of the world.

"Okay, so no Montgomerys or Bradys. I think there are probably a few other single men that our guys might know, though," Dakota said, looking down at her pad of paper.

"How about we draw the line at people not related to the Bradys? Your men can know of them," I said, knowing a headache would be coming along at any moment. That, of course, made me think of Nate, and I pressed my lips together. I couldn't believe that he'd gotten so hurt, and I had no idea. It shouldn't have surprised me that he'd had major life moments without me, but the idea that he'd almost died from what sounded like a horrible accident, and I'd never even known, made me feel something that I wasn't sure I was ready to deal with.

"That's a good caveat," Paris added. "Mostly because the guys seem to know a lot of people. And we don't want to cut off the entire Boulder area because of your arbitrary rules."

I narrowed my eyes. "I don't know if you're making fun of me or agreeing with my rules," I said slowly.

Paris shrugged, looking at her big planner and the notebook she had stuck in there with some magnetic clip thing that I didn't understand. The woman had gone full tilt into the planner world, and I had a feeling if Paris ever changed her career, she could probably have a planner empire.

"It can be both." Paris smiled.

That made me laugh. "I went on one date. I guess that counts for something."

"Of course, it counts," Dakota said.

"You and Hazel didn't have to go on multiple dates with different people."

"Ours were special circumstances," Hazel added.

"Plus, I never actually met the guy I was supposed to go on a date with."

"He's a great guy," Paris said, and we all looked at her. She shrugged. "What? He is."

"However, since he's currently back with his ex-wife, we don't need to add him to any of my lists."

"True. I was just thinking of the what-ifs…" Paris trailed off, and Hazel snorted.

"You mean what if I had gone on a date with that man? Then I wouldn't be with Cross, most likely. And that means you wouldn't be with Prior, and Dakota wouldn't be with Macon. But sure, let's think about what would have happened if I'd gone on a date with…what's his name?"

"It doesn't matter. And I don't like that." Dakota paused. "You being the first one to meet a Brady brother changed everything."

The hot tea splashed over the side of my cup, and I cursed.

"Are you okay?" Dakota asked, helping me clean up my spill.

Paris gave me a weird look. "You're never sloppy. What's wrong?" she asked.

I shook my head, ignoring her. They didn't need to dive into why I felt guilty. Maybe Nate and I had been wrong. Perhaps we should tell them the truth about our past. But what good would it do? I wasn't sure it would do any good, other than to maybe keep some of this guilt off my shoulders. Or perhaps it would stress me out more than I already was and give me even more guilt. It wasn't as if Nate and I were going to pick up where we left off. So, it didn't matter what our past was. And we weren't lying. Not really. We were simply keeping part of the truth out of our daily conversations.

"Anyway, while Nate is a wonderful person, we're not going on another date," I said, trying not to trip over my words. I still hated him, even if I was forced to spend time with him. He had broken my trust and had changed the way I thought of myself. So, no, I would never be his number one fan. And I never wanted to go out on another date with him.

"I can't believe Nate was a dud."

"Is it Nate or Nathaniel?" Paris asked. "I've always wanted to know, and it just never came up."

"It's actually Nathan." I froze as the other women looked at me.

"How do you know that?" Hazel asked, studying me closely. I did my best to look nonchalant.

"You made me go on a date with the man. I picked up on a couple things."

"It looks like the two of you talked, at least." Dakota shrugged. "Maybe it wasn't too bad."

"For a woman who pushed away from the idea of

dating more than any of us did," I began, "you sure are pushy now."

"You pushed just as hard to get me to go in that direction," Dakota said tightly, even though her tone was still sweet.

"Maybe. And I won't say I regret it because look how happy you guys are. But perhaps I didn't need to push that hard."

Paris snorted. "You're only saying that because you're on the other side now."

"That is the truth." I laughed. "However, Nate and I are just friends." I swallowed hard at the lie and hoped the others didn't notice.

Dakota nodded. "That's fine. As long as you can get along while we're hanging out with the group. We will find you the perfect someone. And when Nate finds someone for himself, we can expand our group."

I ignored the slight twinge of jealousy at that thought. I did not want to go out on a date with Nate. I did not want to be jealous of him finding romance with someone else. I might feel a twinge of jealousy, but that didn't make it real. It was probably indigestion.

"I still can't believe you set us up and lied to both of us."

"It wasn't a lie," Paris said quickly.

"It sure as hell felt like one," I argued.

"It wasn't," Hazel said. "Nate needs to get out, too. I think the brothers are starting to feel sorry for him. Mostly because he's always been the most connected of the bunch to women and their feelings."

I froze, wondering what she meant by that. "Excuse me?" I asked.

Once again, Hazel studied me, giving me a weird look. "He's Arden's twin. He's always understood her differently. Better. At least, that's what Cross told me. And from what I've seen when they interact, he's always understood women a bit more than the rest of them. They've all said so, too."

I had fallen for that, hadn't I? The lure of how he seemed to understand everything that I was thinking. Even if it had been a lie. If he had truly understood me, he wouldn't have said the words he did.

I let out a breath. "Okay, who's next?"

"You sound eager all of a sudden."

I ignored the curiosity in Paris's words.

"Let's get it over with," I said.

"Now that's the Myra we know and love."

I was ready for my next step. Because the more I tried, the farther away I could get from Nate. And in the end, that was all that mattered.

"BRIAN, what is it that you do again?" I asked, looking across the table at the man in front of me. I took a sip of my club soda and lime, wishing it was wine. But I planned to have a glass of wine with dinner, so I didn't want more than one while out with a person I had never met before.

Everything was a bit scary because I was on a date with a stranger.

I hadn't thought too much about it before during my dinner with Nate. But now that I knew I would never be on a date with him again, any sense of familiarity was gone.

"I work with Paris. You know that," he said, smiling at me with his perfectly white teeth, his eyes a delicate hazel. At least he had kept his gaze above my chest line. I'd put that in the plus column. Most men couldn't keep their eyes off my ass or my tits. Yes, I had curves, but I didn't want the world to look at only them.

"Oh, I know. But I know she and Prior do completely different things even when they work on the same projects. I just wanted to know what you did."

He smiled again, perfectly pleasant.

He *was* pleasant. He had a friendly, soothing tone. He didn't stare too long or venture onto any topics that could become perilous.

He was entirely sensible.

And I was bored out of my mind.

For all I knew, it was me. Brian would probably have a great time with anybody else. He'd likely laugh it up, tell jokes, and give the girl tingles to the point where she'd want to crawl across the table and rip his tie right off his body.

That was not going to happen with me.

Maybe it *was* me. Perhaps I was the dud and not the man in front of me.

But as he began droning on about programming in a monotone, I was terrified that maybe it was both of us.

I didn't know what had happened. I used to be good at dating. Not only before Nate but also after him. I had never been one to shy away from or hide from the opposite sex. If I wanted to go out on a date, I did. Men asked me out all the time.

Or rather, they used to. Now, guys hit on me awkwardly or made me feel like they didn't want to get too close because I was the icy bitch queen.

I had to stop that.

I needed to be more personable.

But right now, I was genuinely bored.

And I hated it.

"That's so interesting," I said as Brian finished his explanation.

He smiled softly and shook his head. "It's not. My job is tedious, but I love it."

That made me pause. "You can love what you do and still find it tedious?" I asked, confused. I didn't like to do boring things. I did the tasks I needed to do that weren't the most energetic or interesting. Yet I didn't know if I could ever do those tasks for my livelihood. I had walked away from the things that had been set out in front of me and had found true joy even if I was having problems with my current project.

"I don't know if I'm saying it quite right," Brian began. "I enjoy what I do. But I know that not everybody does. I love playing with numbers and trying to find answers. But at the end of the day, I have to look at a specific number and decide if that is the right one or not compared to all the other ones next to it."

"That can be fun, I guess. It's like a puzzle."

He smiled, and once again looked perfectly pleasant. Why couldn't I have feelings for him? "A monotonous one, according to most people. But that's fine by me. I enjoy making the mundane fun."

That made me smile. It didn't sound boring.

"And after a long day of that, coming home to my stamp collection is what makes my days. That and puzzles. You were right. I do like puzzles."

I held back a groan. I liked puzzles, too. But I didn't sound that enthusiastic when I talked about them.

Dinner came, and we enjoyed a satisfying meal—

me a light pasta dish with capers and other seasonings. He ordered buttered noodles and chicken without salt. I wasn't even sure there was any seasoning in the butter.

Brian was bland. Completely dull. And so was his meal.

I wondered what would happen if I shook the pepper at him. Would he sneeze, or would he run away in fear?

I inwardly groaned. I was back to being the icy bitch queen again, if only in my thoughts.

We talked about nothing in particular, and I smiled, trying to sound interested. But I wasn't. And I hated myself a little bit.

After dinner, we split the check, and it just reminded me of Nate, and what I had told him. The fact that I hadn't let Brian pay because it hadn't felt like a real date should have grated. Instead, I only thought of my ex.

And I did not like that. I didn't like that Nathan was always on my mind.

"I wanted to say thank you," Brian said, his hands behind his back as he nodded at me.

"No, thank you for a wonderful night," I added.

"I appreciate you dealing with Boring Brian," he added dryly.

I blinked up at him, confused. "What do you mean?" I asked.

"I know the nicknames I've been given my entire life. I *am* boring, but as I said, I like what I do. So, thank you for sticking with me the whole night and being pleasant and wonderful. But I think we both know this isn't going to work out for us. You need someone and something a little spicier. And I need the same."

He gave me a nod before walking away, and I couldn't help but wonder if he had attacked me.

He needed spicier? He didn't even like spice on his food. Wait, did that mean I was bland, too? Did he not want two lackluster people alone in the same room?

I let out a slight growl, grateful that he couldn't hear me.

Would that spice him up?

I went to my car, threw my bag onto the passenger seat and then winced because it was a lovely bag, and I didn't want to scratch the leather. When I turned on the engine, I did my best not to peel out of the parking lot. Would a sad person speed out of the parking lot in a very nice Audi?

Only if they were trying to make a point.

"What is wrong with me?" I muttered.

I made my way home, annoyed with myself. I was

not bland. I was in a blind date pact with three of my friends. Unexciting people didn't do things like that. But maybe if I hadn't been mundane to begin with, it wouldn't have been necessary. Perhaps I would have been able to find somebody without needing help. Clearly, I was the problem. I hadn't been pushing people away for my entire life—they were running away.

When I got home, I slid off my shoes but kept the dress on. It was a slightly more demure outfit than the one I had worn for Nate. No. The one that I had worn for myself on a date that ended up being with Nate. There was a difference.

I went to my wine fridge, pulled out a bottle, and poured myself an enormous glass. I was halfway done with it when I got a text from Dakota.

Dakota: *Did I leave my Tupperware for the cupcakes at your place?*

Me: *Yes, do you need it? I can drop it off.*

Dakota: *No, you're on your date. I'm sorry.*

Dakota: *Wait. You're on your date. Why are you answering your texts?*

Me: *Brian was a dud. And so am I. Do you need me to drop off the Tupperware?*

I looked at my glass of wine and figured if I stopped now, I could still drive. Or Uber over there and back.

Dakota: *No, I can send someone for it. Thank you so much. And we'll get you another date. I'm sorry!*

She sent a bunch of heart emojis, and I sighed, setting my phone down on the counter. I took another sip of my wine and wondered how I was doing this.

When had it gotten this bad?

Sure, it had been a long time since I had found true happiness or even some semblance of it. But I wasn't dull. I wasn't a dud. Or maybe I was. The fact that I couldn't tell anymore was further evidence that I was completely lost.

I pulled out Dakota's Tupperware and set it next to the front door, waiting for Macon to pick it up. I knew Dakota had an outing the next day for Joshua's class, and I felt terrible that I had kept the cupcake container. I should have dropped it off before now. But I had forgotten, too lost in my memories and work.

The doorbell rang, and I took another sip of my wine, walking over to the front door to let Macon in.

But when I opened it, it wasn't Macon.

No, it was *him*.

"Hey, there," Nate said, sticking his hands into his pockets. "I was over mooching dinner when Dakota said that she needed this ASAP for Joshua's class. So, I figured I'd pick it up for her as payment for the meal."

"Oh. I didn't know it'd be you."

His gaze raked over me, and I ignored the answering chill.

Why couldn't Brian do that for me? Why hadn't a single look from my date given me any type of feeling like Nate gave me now?

And the shudder wasn't revulsion. It should be. But, no, he made me feel sexy, like a woman. As if I were wanted.

And I hated him for it.

"Here you go," I said, handing over the Tupperware. "Tell Dakota I'm sorry for keeping it so long."

"She said she left it. It wasn't like you were holding it hostage." He paused and then cleared his throat. "How was your date?"

I narrowed my eyes at him and then did my best to count to ten. We had a truce, after all. "It was fine. I'm home now. But you never know about date two."

He raised a single brow. "Sounds like fun."

"Anyway, thanks for picking this up for her. I'm about to chug the rest of this wine, so driving probably wouldn't have been a good idea."

"That bad, huh?"

"I'm not going to talk about my date with you, Nate." *For multiple reasons.*

"Understood. I don't think it's a good idea either. I am sorry it didn't go well, though. And I'm only guessing it didn't because of the wine."

I didn't know why he had added that part, but for some reason, I was grateful he had. Maybe the wine was getting to me. We stood there staring at each other awkwardly for a few minutes until he cleared his throat.

"Anyway, I should get this back to her. You look good, Myra."

Surprised, I nearly took a step back. "Oh. Thank you. I tried."

"You never really have to," he whispered. His voice was so low, I wasn't even sure I had heard him. But when he turned on his heel and walked away, I could only stand there blinking, wondering if maybe it was the wine.

Because Nate couldn't have said that.

Did I want him to?

Chapter 4

Nate

I RUBBED MY TEMPLES AND THEN OPENED ANOTHER browser to search a word. I loved my job, I did, but there were only so many days I could spend staring at a screen without wanting to scratch my eyes out. I was a freelance copywriter, but I still had a boss for part of my work because a big publisher employed me. And since I wanted to keep on their payroll because they were my highest paying client, I had to work on this deadline, even if I was past the number of hours they had agreed to.

Though maybe I wasn't paying attention enough.

Perhaps it had nothing to do with the project in front of me. No, it likely had to do with my inability to concentrate on anything but seeing Myra alone, drinking wine while wearing that dress of hers.

It hadn't showcased as many of her curves or shown as much cleavage as the other dress she had worn, but this one had been a little clingier, made her look a little softer.

And yet, the idea that I knew she had sexy-as-fuck curves under that dress and was hiding it made it even hotter somehow.

What the fuck was wrong with me?

I finished looking up the word and took a few notes. I was done for the day. I put away my work and figured I would wrap it up. I'd have to do a few pages over the weekend, but that was fine. I usually worked, if only for a few hours.

My job paid well, and the settlement I'd gotten from the accident had given me a decent savings account so I didn't have to worry about my house or my bills. But if I wanted to grow my retirement or pay for medical insurance or have money to go out with my family and friends, I needed to work.

I put away my computer and got up from my chair, rolling my shoulders back. I worked strategically in different places around the house, but never in my bedroom. I remembered my mom saying that I was never allowed to do homework in bed. I always thought it was a weird thing, but she explained that the more we studied or worked in bed, the harder it became to fall asleep because it stopped being our safe place to relax.

I completely understood that now. And while I knew that my sister, Arden, occasionally worked from bed because of her lupus, I tried not to do it. That meant I had comfy chairs with lumbar support in every room, so I never got bored. It was the little things in life. And maybe if I kept thinking about chairs and backaches, I wouldn't think about Myra and that dress.

She was dating. Hell, *I* was dating. I had gone out thanks to my brothers, and it wasn't my fault that the date had ended up being with Myra. So what if she wasn't the person I had been expecting? That didn't mean I needed to focus on that. Right?

She was allowed to date whoever she wanted, and I was allowed to do the same with whoever I felt like being with. After all, she had likely been with plenty of men while we were apart.

I grumbled at that thought. But hell, I had been with several women since, too. I'd even had a serious girlfriend since Myra. So, fuck that. I didn't need to get jealous. Sure, she was hot. She always had been, and she still was. Good for her.

That didn't mean I had to want her. I was so

tangled up in that, I feared I would give myself another headache.

I went to the kitchen and got myself one of my reusable water bottles and chugged a third of it before my doorbell rang. I frowned, looked at the clock, and then went over to open the door.

My family stood on the other side: Arden, Prior, Macon, and Cross. If my parents weren't living out of state, they probably would have been there, as well.

"To what do I owe the pleasure?" I asked dryly as I stepped back, not bothering to invite them in. They would come in on their own anyway. That's what family did. And I was exactly like them.

"We just wanted to see how you were doing," Arden said, rising to her tiptoes to kiss my jaw. I hugged her tightly, laying a kiss on the top of her head and making sure my twin went right to the couch to sit down. She'd had a rough go of it last week, and though I knew she was fine and hadn't been admitted to the hospital for kidney issues, it had come close.

Lupus was no joke, and I hated that she had to deal with her health daily when I didn't. Yes, I had some issues thanks to the accident, but it was nowhere near my sister's struggles. She was my twin, and I hated that I couldn't take her pain away.

"You're giving me that look again. Stop feeling

bad. I'm doing great. You know Liam wouldn't let me out of the house if I weren't having a good day."

I snorted at the thought of my brother-in-law. "You know, you're right. I kind of like him these days."

"You're only saying that because he's on your side right now. If you were thinking about him and his precious baby sister, you wouldn't."

I scowled, and the rest of my brothers started groaning about something or other. "There, I don't like him anymore." I laughed.

"I see you're not working since your laptop is stowed. That means I can rummage through your fridge for something to eat," Prior said, rubbing his hands together.

"What the hell?" I asked, laughing. "Why didn't you guys just bring snacks if you wanted to eat while you were here doing…whatever it is you're doing?"

Prior grinned. "We could have, but it's better to eat your snacks."

I heard barking from the other room, and I grinned and went over to where Daisy was currently on her back paws, trying to get out of the octagon gate I had put up for her. She was still a puppy, and we had played hard earlier. Plus, she had gone for a long walk. Leash training was no joke. She was part Golden Retriever, part something else, though the vet I had talked to thought it was some kind of Collie. Macon and I agreed. I didn't care. All I knew was that I was in love with my puppy.

"I was going to ask where our favorite niece is." Macon pushed me out of the way and picked up Daisy, cradling her in his arms.

"I thought that was my puppy," I said, a little hurt.

"But she's so happy to see her favorite uncle," Macon said, letting her lick his chin. I followed Macon out to the backyard to let Daisy do her business. We gave her cheers and then took her back inside for water and a treat.

"Puppy training looks to be going well." Arden laughed, on her knees now as Daisy said hello.

"She's a little nippy, so be careful," I warned.

"Make sure you have a toy near if she starts to get chewy." Macon handed over a key ring with a pacifier-type thing. It was one of her favorite toys, to the point that I had one upstairs and another downstairs.

"I'm seriously in love with this baby." Arden ran her hands through Daisy's soft, rust-colored fur.

"Are you going to get another one to go with your Jasper?" I asked, speaking of her white Siberian Husky.

Arden shook her head. "No. We're working on the whole baby thing first."

"And having a puppy and a baby might not be great, at least not at the same time."

"I have a feeling Jasper's going to be amazing with whoever we get," Arden began. "However, I don't want to overwhelm him. Or us, to be honest. It's a long process, and we're not even trying for only a baby. We know the waitlist for that takes forever, and children in homes are waiting for us, too. We know that. So, we're taking our time. Until then, it's just the three of us."

Daisy licked Arden's face before moving to go cuddle Cross on the floor. My siblings and I sat on the tile as Daisy moved between all of us, her tail wagging, looking excited that everybody was here for her. And now that I thought about it, my siblings could be here for her and not me. Honestly, I wouldn't blame them. I loved my dog. I had thought about getting one for a while, and since my brother was a vet, he was the best one to go to. Daisy had been in the shelter, a little too hyperactive for the young family who had initially bought her. She had been an accident between two breeders, and I wasn't a fan of the fact that they had tossed her to the curb.

Macon was looking into if anything could be done, but it didn't matter in the end. I had a new puppy who was the best thing in my life, and I had my work. And my family. What else did a guy need?

Myra in that dress filled my mind again, and I held back a curse.

"So, I guess we're setting you up on another date?" Prior asked, carefully not looking at me.

"Since the first date you sent me on was a bust, sure."

"Hey," Arden said, and I winced. Arden knew exactly why dating Myra wasn't a good idea. But she wasn't telling anybody, and neither was I. The fact that my twin had held onto this secret for so long hurt. Not because it was her fault, but because I had forced her to lie to everybody. Myra and I needed to do something about that. But I didn't know what problems it would solve if we finally told everybody. If anything, it might bring about more of them.

Macon played with Daisy as he spoke. "So, Myra's oh for two in the date department."

"That's what I hear," I said.

"You met with Myra again?" Cross asked, seeming curious.

I shrugged, acting like it was no big deal. Because it wasn't. "Of course. Didn't Macon tell you? I had to stop by her house to pick up something for Dakota. She'd recently gotten home from her date and was drinking a huge glass of wine."

Macon winced. "Hell. I didn't know about the wine. Was the guy mean? Do we need to do something?"

I shook my head. "No. I don't think so." I froze. "Shit. Maybe the girls should talk to her."

Why was I so protective? I shouldn't be. Myra had hurt me. I didn't need to care about her. No, that was a lie. I had loved her once. Just because we weren't together anymore, and she me didn't mean I wanted her to be in pain or have to deal with assholes.

Fuck that. I wasn't a horrible person. At least, I didn't think so.

"Anyway, now that you have Daisy, you have someone in your life," Prior said, and Arden slapped his shoulder.

"Be nice, or I'll tell Paris that you were mean."

Prior's eyes widened. "Please don't."

"Afraid of the little missus?" I asked.

"I'm totally going to tell Paris that you called her the little missus," Prior added drily.

I cringed. "Okay, fine. What's said here does not go home to your other halves."

"I can't promise that," Cross said. "I'm not going to promise that at all."

"Fine," I grumbled.

I did not want to feel jealous about the fact that they all had someone to go home to. They could talk to someone who cared about what they were feeling and what they needed.

I didn't have that. But I did have Daisy. My girl

licked my chin and then curled into a ball in my lap, promptly falling asleep.

"She's too cute," Arden whispered, reaching out to run her hand over Daisy's nose.

"Yeah. And she's all mine."

"Put her back in her octagon on her little bed. That way, she knows she has a safe place."

I nodded at Macon and did as he suggested before washing my hands and going back to the living room where everyone else had gone.

"I like that you can see her area from your couch," Cross said.

I smiled. "I move it around depending on where I'm at. I want her to know that I'm here, but I also don't want her to become too dependent."

Macon nodded. "That's a problem for a lot of puppy owners. As soon as Mom or Dad leaves, they whine and freak out."

"Crate training sucks." I sighed as I rubbed my temple.

"Is your head okay?" Arden asked, taking my hand.

"It's fine. I was wearing my blue light glasses earlier, but then I took them off to go for a walk with Daisy and forgot to put them back on."

"You know better than that," Arden chided.

"I do. And I'll be better. Promise."

"Here, this will help." Prior handed me one of my beers.

"Oh, thanks. So, we're going to drink the entire six-pack?" I asked.

"You've got it." Arden took a bottle for herself.

"Should you be drinking?"

She flipped me off. "I'm allowed to have a beer, asshole."

"I worry."

"I worry about you, too. So much that I'm going to help in this whole blind date thing that the brothers put you up for without consulting me."

"We didn't know if you would like it."

"I'm not sure if I do, but I want to be part of it," she said to Cross.

"I want to make sure Nate is as happy as the rest of us."

"Thank you for making me feel like a pity project," I grumbled.

"But you're our pity project," Arden said with a laugh.

I flipped her off and then took a sip of my beer.

"Just, whatever you do, make sure it's not Myra again please?" I asked, doing my best not to look at Arden as I said it.

"Why?" Macon asked.

"I don't know why you set us up in the first place.

We're allowed to be friends and nothing more. And it's not like you and Dakota, where the girls set you up so you could talk out your feelings before Dakota went on a real date. Myra wants true happiness and a future and all that shit."

I hated the words even as I said them, but I knew they were true.

"And she can't have that with you?" Cross asked casually.

Was it too nonchalant? What did he know?

Again, I didn't look at Arden.

"Let's make sure Myra and I can figure out how to be friends. I don't mind going on another date. Eventually. Only not with her."

"I think you protest too much," Prior said, taking another sip of his beer.

"And I think I could probably still take you. I can't take Cross or Macon, especially since Macon's been boxing. But I can take your scrawny ass."

"Just don't break the beer bottles. If you do, I'll be the one cleaning it up. Like always," Arden said, and I shook my head, holding back a laugh.

"So, you're not taking my side? You're my twin. You don't think I can take him?" I asked.

"I want no part of this. Because I think you're all weird. But I love you."

"And we love you," I said, kissing her on the top of the head.

"Oh, thank you," she said, snuggling into my side. "And I will help you find the perfect date. Because you deserve happiness, Nate. Although, we may have to do something about that haircut of yours."

I gasped as my brothers laughed. I knew she was teasing me. They all were. It's what we did. And as they went over who might want to go on a date with me, I did my best not to think about Myra. Something that was getting harder and harder to do these days.

I hated the idea that I couldn't get her out of my head.

Again.

Chapter 5

Nate

BEFORE

I WAS LATE. *Seriously late. But if I weren't careful, I would end up passed out and late. Nobody wanted that.*

I cringed as I looked at the line outside of Starbucks and then glanced around the commons, wondering if there was another coffee shop near. I had been on this campus for two years, but I couldn't think of a single place to get coffee that might not have a line.

Could I have had coffee at my house? Absolutely.

Could I have picked up coffee on my way here? No doubt.

But I could not find any memory of thinking of that while on my way to campus.

I needed caffeine. It was the only way I was going to make it through organic chemistry.

Organic chemistry was made for people who thought they liked math and science, and then they put it all in this weird combination of things that apparently had to do with electrons. I didn't know.

I just needed to memorize my reactions so I could pass my test and move on to more important things.

Like anything other than organic chemistry.

"Damn it," I mumbled, looking down at my phone to check the time.

I had five minutes until class started, and if you weren't on time, Mr. Augustine did not let you in. Oh, he might keep the doors open and didn't nail them shut, but he made sure you got shamed for daring to walk into his class late. And he didn't put notes online, didn't share his slides.

You had to read the textbook before class started, do all of the worksheets and questionnaires beforehand, and then come in to learn what you'd already pretty much taught yourself. However, it wasn't like you could teach yourself that because everything was too complicated, and you needed him to explain it.

In other words, it was the worst way to take an organic chemistry class. Next time, I was just going to Metro where I knew Dr. Thomas was.

That was a good idea. I would get coffee here and then walk to my advisor to drop out of this organic chemistry class and use one of my transfer credits to take a class at Metro.

Yes, that was brilliant.

Only it was also stupid.

I didn't have time in my busy class load to change my schedule like that. I had to get organic chemistry out of the way this semester so I could move on to other things. Being an EMT wasn't going to be easy, but I couldn't let this class and my lack of caffeine stop me.

Determined, I turned on my heel, knowing I'd just have to deal without the coffee. The soft body that ran into me felt like heaven, and I cursed.

She hit the ground in front of me, and I blinked down at her, trying to make my mind catch up to what I saw.

A beautiful woman with blond hair, wide eyes, and killer curves glared at me from the ground where she lay, the contents of her messenger bag strewn around the pavement, and her eyes, initially wide and beautiful, now narrowed into slits.

Though still gorgeous.

"Are you kidding me?" the girl said before scrambling to her feet. I reached down to help her up, and she slapped at my hand.

"No, we already know you copped a feel. That's enough."

Given I had done no such thing, I blinked at her. Others whispered around us, and I winced.

"I didn't. At least I don't think so. I'm sorry. Here, let me help you pick that up."

She slapped my hand again, and I winced.

"No need to hit me."

"You've done enough of that for both of us, haven't you?" she said before stuffing all of her things into her bag. "It's going to take me forever to organize this the way I want it." She rolled her shoulders back and sighed. "Thanks for that."

"I'm seriously sorry."

"Sure, you are."

Then she sauntered off, and I couldn't help but watch how her ass moved as she walked away.

"Damn, I'd like a piece of that," the guy beside me said, and I frowned.

"Hey, be nice."

"You're the one checking out her ass and copping a feel."

"I didn't," I said, my cheeks reddening.

"Whatever you say. Just be careful, women these days don't like it when you look up their skirts and shit. The female movement and whatever."

The guy, who had to be at least twenty-five, rolled his eyes, pushed his hair back from his face, and walked away, hacky sack in hand. Were hacky sacks even popular anymore? What did it matter? It was Colorado. He was likely stoned, and hacky sacks were probably the thing he was best at.

And now I was going to be seriously late. And I still didn't have caffeine. But I did have the image and feel of a woman with curves that would haunt my memory for ages to come.

I ignored the taunting jeers from my fellow classmates, my professor, and my TA as I finally made my way to class and was forced to sit up front. That's where all the late students were placed.

I pulled out my notebook and took copious notes, hoping to hell I'd be able to understand them later.

Damn, I needed a fucking cup of coffee.

And I needed to get that girl out of my head. I hadn't even asked her name. Sure, I might know what she felt like up against me now, but that didn't matter. I would never see her again. And that was fine with me.

As soon as class ended, I piled my things into my bag, waved off a friend, and practically ran to the coffee place.

Thankfully, I was somehow first in line. We were between breaks, and the organic chemistry class went a little longer than others. I got a venti triple shot macchiato and nearly chugged it, ignoring the burn on my tongue.

I turned the corner and cursed as the coffee slopped over the rim of my cup onto my shirt, and I nearly ran into someone.

Again.

I looked down at the girl and let out a laugh. "Oh, you."

She looked up at me and tilted her head. "You. You need to watch where you're going."

"Maybe. However, fancy meeting you here again."

"Really? That's the line you're going with? Fancy meeting you here?"

"We've run into each other twice in one day. It has to mean something."

"It means that we have a similar class schedule on the north side of campus, and both of us needed caffeine."

I looked down at her empty hands. "I don't see any caffeine."

"I've been trying to get some all day and haven't been able to. But thank you for that."

"Here, let me buy you a cup. I could probably use a second one."

She studied my face. "We better hurry or we're going to end up at the end of a long line."

"You're not going to say no?" I asked with a laugh.

"I want coffee. You're offering to pay. I'm fine with that. As long as you realize that this doesn't mean I'm going to sleep with you."

I nearly choked. "Oh, uh… I didn't, uh… You know, never mind."

"I take it you're not an English major?" she asked, and I nearly sniped back before I saw the laughter in her eyes.

"Drama, actually. I want to be an actor." I made sure I said, actor *in a snotty, fake British accent, and her eyes widened for a fraction of a second before she laughed.*

"I'm sorry, I had a really hard economics test today, and I hated it. Why do I need to know economics?"

I shook my head. "I don't know, other than it's a general requirement, probably because it helps make the world go 'round."

"Maybe. And if I want to own my own business someday, I guess I need to know it."

I studied her face, wanting to know more. "So, you're a business major?"

"No. I'm an economics major," she said, and I nearly tripped again.

"And you hate it?"

"I'm a freshman. Apparently, when you're seventeen and not allowed to fill out your forms without your mom and dad signing them, you don't get to pick your major."

I ignored the sad twinge that she was only seventeen. Down, boy. *"Oh, well, I guess you're super smart for getting in early."*

She shook her head. "I'm eighteen now. I have a summer birthday. That means I get screwed out of some things. But I'm an adult now, and I'm taking the classes that I want. Even if my parents decided to move to this state to be near me for the semester."

My eyes widened at that. "Your parents were able to move here for a semester? From where?"

"California. I know, I know. They're super overprotective and always in my business. It's probably why I haven't ever had a serious boyfriend." Her eyes widened, and her cheeks flushed. It made her look really pretty.

"What is your name, by the way? I'm Nate. Nathan. But I go by Nate."

"I like both. I might just have to call you Nathan. At least, you know, if I ever see you again." She laughed. "I'm Myra. Sorry. I'm not good at this whole human interaction thing. Or maybe I used to be and then moving out here where the air is

really thin made me realize that I had no idea what I was doing."

I laughed, and we went to the front of the line. I let her order and got a second macchiato for myself. I would be jittery as hell by the end of the day, but I didn't mind.

And I had a feeling that maybe the jitters didn't come from the coffee. Perhaps they were from the girl at my side.

"ARE YOU KIDDING ME? *How do you know that?" Myra said, stealing a dumpling from my plate.*

I tapped her hand with my chopstick, but she was too fast for me, so I stole a crab rangoon from hers.

"Hey, that was mine."

"No, you ate my dumpling, so this is mine. To answer your question, I knew the answer to that because I took that class last semester. Same professor and everything. Tests are different, though, so I can't help you there."

Myra shook her head. "I wouldn't accept them anyway. I'm not a cheat."

I held up my hands, chopsticks and all. "Sorry, I didn't mean to insinuate you were. I'm just used to saying shit like that because many of the people around here want the easy way out."

"I may hate my major and will likely change soon, but I don't want the easy way out. I want to learn. I want to do things. I want to be somebody."

I leaned down and captured her lips with mine, sinking into her. She was soft and sweet and gentle. And she made me think of happiness and a future. I didn't know why, I knew we were too young, and that everything was going way too fast, but I was falling in love with Myra.

And my family would rip into me if they ever found out.

"I thought we were supposed to be studying and finishing our dinner," Myra whispered against my lips.

"If that's what you want to do," I grumbled, and then she kissed me harder.

My pulse raced, and I set down the chopsticks so I could cup her face with my hands.

"I want to, Nathan," she whispered, her voice soft, sweet but also sure.

"We don't have to do anything you don't want to do. We can wait."

"I'm not a virgin, Nathan. Neither are you. I want to be with you."

"Okay," I whispered and kissed her again.

I led her down to the couch, taking it slow, running my hands up and down her body as she did the same with mine, both of us learning each other. We had nearly gone this far before, still feeling like this was new, as if the times we had been with others hadn't prepared us for what this was.

This had to mean something—the seriousness of it all. Only, I didn't know what.

I kissed her softly, needing her, bringing her closer to the edge.

And when I slipped inside her, we both moaned. Her hands clutched my body, and my hips nestled against hers. And then we moved, arching into each other as if we had never been like this before. And maybe we hadn't.

Perhaps this was exactly what we had been missing.

Maybe this was precisely what we each needed.

"I love you," I whispered.

Her eyes widened, and I nearly cursed at myself for saying the words.

Tears slid down her cheeks as she arched into me and kissed me again.

"I love you."

And then we shattered.

"I CANNOT BELIEVE *we're doing spring break in Vegas," Myra said, laughing.*

"Everyone else is doing it." I laughed.

"At least you're nearly twenty-one. I'm not even close."

"Nearly *twenty-one doesn't really help in Vegas. But we can still hang out at the pool and see the Hoover Dam and things."*

"And we can do…other things," Myra said, and my cock hardened.

Apparently, having a girlfriend on spring break would be

kick-ass, unlike what my friends had said as they razzed me before they went off to find women for themselves at the pool.

"I don't think we're going to need to leave the hotel room often," I said, and she grinned.

"Oh, so we're just going to watch movies?"

"Maybe. And you know Dave got us some vodka for the room. That way, we don't have to go out." I whispered the words in case others overheard, and she smiled again.

"Okay, I trust you."

Warmth filled me. "Yeah?"

"Of course, I do. I wouldn't be here if I didn't."

Everything was moving so fast. It felt like I had known her for my entire life. Like I would die without her. I could barely breathe, overwhelmed by the desire to be with her.

So, I kissed her, taking her in.

I still wanted more.

"Let's get married," I blurted. She looked up at me, her eyes wide.

"What?" she asked.

"Did I say those words out loud?" I queried, my heart racing.

"Married? Are you serious? We've only been together for like six months. I haven't even met your family yet since they're all up north and I went home for the holidays."

"Yeah, that was stupid. I mean, we're in Vegas, but you know, it should take more than one night before we even drink for us to get married."

"You really want to get married?"

"Why not?" I asked, the idea making sense now, even though I knew it was idiotic. "We both want the same things in life. We want a future. And you know I love you. What's stopping us?"

"Everything is," she said, but then she frowned, looking down at her hands. "Or maybe, nothing is. This could be ours. No one else's. A decision that we make. One that no one can take away from us."

I looked down at her, my pulse thudding so hard in my ears I could barely hear anything else. "Married. You and me. We can do this. We can figure out everything else later, but we can get this done now, just you and me. No big brothers or overbearing families telling us what to do."

"Married."

"I love you, Myra."

"And I love you, Nathan. So, yes. I'll marry you."

I KNEW *a person's heart could break. I had read it before. I didn't know that it could shatter into a thousand pieces as you tried to keep up.*

You weren't supposed to realize that the fate you had set out for yourself was a lie. I thought that making stupid decisions when young was something people did. I didn't know I would be the one jumping headfirst into secrets and denial.

I swallowed hard, trying to keep the bile back, my whole body shaking. I felt like I was two steps behind.

I looked down at the photos, at the people in front of me, and couldn't breathe.

The love of my life, my wife, *lay in bed with another man, a smile on her face, both of them naked and clearly sated after whatever the hell they had done together in bed.*

"Why are you showing this to me?" I asked, my voice breaking. It hadn't broken like that in so damn long, but I didn't feel like I was in my twenties right now. I felt like I was ten again. Or maybe fifty. I didn't know. I just didn't feel like me.

Myra's parents sat in front of me, sad expressions on their faces, the pearls around Myra's mother's neck bright in the glow of the lights, the crisp suit on her father's body looking as if it had been custom made for him.

I had never met Myra's parents before, but I had married their daughter.

I knew we had made a mistake, had gone too fast. But we had both said that we could figure things out and make it work. However, now that we were back in Colorado, it had only been four days—four days, and everything was wrong.

"We wanted to show you what Myra's boyfriend gave us."

"Boyfriend?" My hands shook. "But I'm her husband."

I didn't miss the tightening of their eyes.

Her mother sighed. "You might have those papers, but you don't have her heart. You can't. I meant her boyfriend from back home, where she belongs. He loves her."

Myra's father tightened his jaw. "He gave us these photos. Ones they must have taken together. Because, as I said, they love each other. And you can see they're recent. At least from the past six months. When you said she was with you."

"She's been with me the whole time…" I trailed off, trying to work through the lies.

"Nathan, I'm sorry."

"My name's Nate." I hated the word from her mouth. The only person that called me Nathan *was Myra. And I never wanted to hear that name again.*

"Okay, Nate,*" her father began again. "We didn't want to see these photos, but they came into our possession. And we didn't know any other way to tell you that Myra has been unfaithful. She's made mistakes. And she needs to go home. To heal. To get her life together. And you need to let her."*

"I don't understand. How did you even hear about any of this?"

His hands tightened in front of me, and I swallowed hard. "Myra has responsibilities, family obligations. We always knew where our daughter was. We thought we would let this relationship run its course, but we were wrong about her true intentions. She's not meant to be with you, Nathan."

"Nate," I bit out.

"I'm sorry," her father said again. "But as you can see, Myra has been lying to you. She's been lying to all of us. We're going to take her out of school. Take her home. Get her some help.

But we thought you needed to know the truth. We are here for you, Nate."

I didn't want to believe them. I knew the photos had to be lies. But the evidence was right in front of me. Myra had cheated on me. I noticed the bracelet on her wrist in the picture. It was the one I had given her for Christmas right before she went back to California. And, apparently, did this.

I thought she had been with me.

"I don't know what to say."

"As I said, we're going to take Myra home now. You need to break up with her. We can get the annulment," her father elaborated. "That is what's needed."

"You can't get an annulment if the marriage is consummated," I said without thinking, and her mother blanched.

"Fine. We can do a divorce here. It doesn't matter. Myra needs help. And you need to let her go. You don't need to get hurt any more than you are."

Betrayal stung, and I felt like I was going to throw up. But I knew somewhere deep down that I had been making a mistake when I had said, "I do." When I told her that I wanted to marry her. We had been drunk on love or lust, and things had moved far too quickly.

It was all a mistake.

"You need to go now," I said.

"Are you going to do the right thing, Nate?" her mother asked.

"Please, just go," I said.

They stared at me for a long while before they finally left, leaving me sitting there wondering what the hell had happened. They'd taken the photos, and I felt like nothing was right. As if nothing were real.

How the hell had this happened?

I knew we had moved too fast, that we needed to take a few steps back and figure out who we were together. But together clearly wasn't something she wanted. Maybe it wasn't something she had ever wanted.

"But why did she say yes, then?" I asked.

That bracelet. The one I had given her.

She'd worn it in that photo with another man.

"Nathan?" Myra asked from the doorway. "I rang the doorbell, but you didn't answer. And the door was open so I came in. Are you okay? What's wrong?" She ran to me, kneeling at my feet, and I looked down at the ring on her finger, the band on mine, the one that I only wore when nobody was home because I wasn't ready to tell my parents that I had gotten married.

I wasn't ready to be married. If I had to lie about it, I knew I wasn't ready. And Myra hadn't been either.

"You need to go," I said, the words out of my mouth before I realized I was even saying them.

"What?" Myra asked. "What's wrong? Is it your dad? Your mom? Oh my God, did you tell them?"

"No, I didn't. I didn't do anything." I looked down at the ring on my finger, then slid it off and stared at it on my palm. "But it seems you've been doing things."

I heard her sharp intake of breath, and knew it had to be the truth. She had to know that she was caught.

My heart lurched, and I felt as if I were falling.

I loved her. But I didn't know her. Not really. So, maybe I only loved the idea of her.

"I saw the photos," I whispered.

"What?"

"You cheated on me. I know you did. You cheated. I don't even know you."

She scrambled to her feet, her head shaking as tears filled her eyes. She always cried when she got angry, but maybe that was a lie, too. Perhaps she was simply a great actress.

"Where are you getting this? Pictures? I've only been with you since we met. It's always only been you. I married you.*"*

I let out a bark of laughter. "Yeah, you married me. In Vegas. Cliché much? It's over, Myra. Take this." I tossed the ring at her, and she caught it, fumbling a bit. "Just go. I'm done."

"Are you kidding me?" she asked. "You're saying it's over? Because of some pictures I haven't seen? And you think I cheated? You know me, Nathan. I would never cheat on you. Where are you getting this?"

"I saw the proof. I know who you are now. I should have known given how everything moved so fast, and you were so readily into it. What else have you been lying about? No, you know what? I don't care. We made a mistake, and we both knew it. Neither of us told anyone in our lives about the marriage, and yet we were supposed to be husband and wife? No, fuck that.

You're a cheater...you cheated on me. You broke my trust. I can't believe anything you say. You need to go."

Her face blanched, and I felt like I might throw up.

She stopped crying and looked at me, blinking. "I don't know what you saw, and I don't know what you think you know. But I would never do that."

"I saw the truth. I don't know you, Myra. I don't think I ever did."

"No, Nathan. I didn't know you.*" She looked down at the ring in her palm and then slid hers off her finger. She clutched them both tightly and swallowed hard.*

"It's over, Myra."

Then she walked out, leaving me thinking maybe I had made a mistake. But, no, I had already made the biggest mistake.

She'd cheated on me. When I trusted her.

But now, she was gone.

We had been too young. Stupid.

And now, we were over.

Chapter 6

Myra

I DID MY BEST NOT TO THINK ABOUT THE TIME BEFORE I moved back to Colorado. It was as if I were a different person then. One that had caught a glimpse of freedom and truth but then had the rug ripped out from under my feet.

Nathan hadn't believed me. After the time we had spent together, the promises we made—even if made hastily—he still hadn't believed me.

And to this day, I didn't know why he had so easily parted ways with me. Or how he had delved into those untruths to follow whatever path he felt he needed to in order to push me away.

He might've felt as if I had betrayed him then, but I knew it was the opposite. He had so easily believed in my failings, yet he had been the one to fail me in the end.

And now, every time I looked at him, I remembered that time. I remembered the pain and anger.

And I hated myself for it. But not as much as I hated him.

We were trying to get past that. To find common ground where we could act like reasonable adults. But it wasn't easy. Especially when, every time I looked at him, I remembered what we'd had, and what he had thrown away with his casual cruelty.

I looked down at my canvas and knew that today wasn't going to be a day for art. Still, I had a commissioned piece coming up that I wanted to focus on, and I needed to get a few sketches down. Later, I could focus on this piece since it was more for fun for an upcoming auction.

I had a showing on my calendar in a few months, and I needed to go through my plans for that, too, but my head wasn't in the right place.

I loved what I did. It wasn't what I'd thought to do—or what I'd thought I'd be *allowed* to do. But once I'd pushed that word from my vocabulary, I had found myself loving what I did even more. Only now, seeing Nathan as much as I had been, routinely pushed me back into the past.

And why did he keep popping back into my mind? I needed to focus on my art, my friends, and anything *but* him.

The girls were going to set me up on another date soon. With someone that wasn't my past haunting me. Maybe if I told them why I couldn't be with Nathan, they would understand. I was just afraid that they would push me away once they learned that I had been hiding such an important fact about myself. I cleaned up my area and then went to the other side of my house that was less studio and a little more me.

I had purchased the place a few years ago when I returned to Colorado. I hadn't finished my economics degree when I was forced to move back to California. But I *had* gotten a business degree. That way, I could run my business, even if my line of work had nothing to do with what my parents wanted me to do.

I worked hard and fell into the *hobby* my mother always joked about. But now I was an artist that people sought out, even if I wasn't at the highest level of the industry as some around me were. But I would get there. Or I would keep trying until I did.

Because this was my passion. And in a world where people's passions were pulled from them so they could focus on what others wanted, I knew I was privileged. I knew the only reason I could work as I did and focus on my art and charities was because of my trust fund. It was because of the privilege I had been raised with.

I pulled my hair from the clip at the back of my head, my blond hair brushing the tops of my shoulders. I had recently cut off a few more inches, and I liked the look, even though I kind of missed being able to braid it over my shoulder.

My house had four bedrooms—one I used for an office, a guest bedroom, and a little reading nook I made for myself. The studio attachment had been for another artist who lived here before I bought the place. It had been like kismet when I found the listing, and I had offered the asking price without a second look.

I was lucky, and I loved my home. It was all light colors, creams with greige, reclaimed wood and metal. It was nothing like the ornate opulence and wealth-induced creativity that I had been born into. My parents had never once set foot into this home. They would hate it. That had only been *part* of my decision to buy it. The idea that this place was just me had been the main reason.

I went to the kitchen to pour myself a glass of water and did my best to calm my nerves so I could focus on what was important. The idea that I was so scatterbrained annoyed me. I wasn't always like this, and I couldn't entirely blame Nathan for it.

I looked around the kitchen and frowned. I needed to do another deep clean. A service came in once a month, but since I lived alone and didn't have pets, I could usually handle everything on my own. It was only when I traveled for work or was busy on a project that I sometimes couldn't quite keep up. Besides, the company I hired was a group of single moms who got together to help younger moms find a place in the world and finish school.

If I could help others while keeping myself sane and my house clean, all the better.

I pulled out my cleaning supplies and began scrubbing counters, cleaning grout, and then started my deep clean of the kitchen. It had been on my to-do list for the weekend, but it seemed I would be working out my frustrations today.

I was elbow deep in cleanser when the doorbell rang. I frowned.

The girls all had plans today, so I knew we weren't meeting, and I didn't know who else it could be. It couldn't be Nathan.

My heart rate sped up.

He had come into my house once before to pick up that container for Dakota. All the other times he had been here, he'd only dropped me off when we took care of Joshua. He claimed it was because he wanted to keep me safe when our friends were in danger, but it was still hard for me to stomach having him so close.

I made my way to the door and looked through the peephole. I froze, not quite believing what I was seeing. I looked at the cleaning clothes I had on, the smell of pine still drifting in the air.

I tried to reach out to grab the doorknob, but my hand slipped. I held back a curse, wiping my palms on my jeans before I opened the door and looked at the three people who had never been at my house before.

My mother looked at least a decade younger than she was. There was no way anyone would think she was in her fifties. I didn't think she had ever had any work done, but for all I knew, she had. If it made her happy, I wouldn't care. But nothing ever made my mother happy. I sure hadn't.

She was a couple of inches taller than I was and wore the perfect shoes for whatever environment she was in. Although, they always had to have a heel to make her calves look great. It was something she had taught me when I was a young girl as I slid my feet into her eight-hundred-dollar shoes and walked around the bedroom. She hadn't laughed with me or encouraged me. She had scolded me and then showed me how to walk in them to accentuate my features and be the perfect young lady.

I shifted my gaze to my father. He had gone gray at the temples and had a frown on his face. That was his normal look, though. It didn't worry me. He always scowled. Nothing was ever good enough for my dad. I hadn't been. Maybe because I wasn't the son he had so desired. He had wanted somebody to carry on the family name. Instead, he had gotten a girl who refused to listen to him and tried to ruin the family name. At least, in his opinion.

I looked over at my cousin, his dark hair brushed back from his face—a thousand-dollar haircut if I guessed correctly. He had on nice slacks, a button-down shirt, and looked his version of casual. Though I knew it was anything but casual given the name brands he wore.

His Ferragamos were perfectly shined as if he hadn't recently walked off a plane and was now in the mountain areas of Boulder, Colorado. The three of them looked so out of place, and I was surprised they even knew where I lived. Maybe they had looked at the return address on the Christmas card I had sent or something. They certainly never sent one back. And I hadn't heard from them since I moved here after finally taking a stand.

"Are you just going to stare at us, or are you going to ask us in?" my mother asked, her voice crisp and still so familiar. I nearly bowed my head and curtsied, but this was my home. I was going to stand up to them.

I had loved my parents once. Had cherished them and did my best to live up to what they needed and wanted of me.

But when I was broken, and they forced me back to California and tried to mold me in their image, I realized I wasn't enough—I had never been.

Even now, I didn't think they thought I was, despite the fact that I knew who I was now.

"I wasn't expecting you."

"Clearly," my father said, his gaze going down to my bare feet, my jeans with the holes in the knee and the thigh, and my T-shirt. I had gone from painting to cleaning, and I looked *my* version of casual.

Which was nothing like my family's.

"Please, come in." I didn't want them inside. I couldn't simply ask them to leave, though. I could, but there was no good reason.

If they were here, it wasn't merely to judge me. No, that would be the icing on the cake. This had to be an emergency. Or they wanted something. Regardless, this was my home. I could dress how I wanted, and after they left, I would call my friends, and we could have a bottle of wine—or four—and I could lament.

I would not let my parents get to me or ruin everything.

"Your home is...nice," Roland, my cousin, said as he looked around, practically bouncing on his feet.

I ignored the sneer in his words. "Thank you. I love it. It fits well into the mountainside."

"It's very rural," my mother remarked. "But quaint."

I nearly rolled my eyes but held myself back. "I was deep-cleaning the kitchen, so I apologize for the scent of cleaning supplies and my appearance. I wasn't expecting you."

"Do you not have a cleaning service for that?" my father asked, disappointment evident in his tone.

"I do, but sometimes I like to do an additional clean so I can clear my head. May I ask what brings you here?" I asked. They narrowed their eyes at me. "Not that it's not a joy to see you, but it's been a few years, and I didn't know you were coming."

"We sent you a certified letter," my mother said, and I frowned.

"I didn't receive it. You could have called. Sent an email. A telegram…" I trailed off.

My father interrupted. "There's no need for that tone."

"Okay, I think we started off on the wrong foot. Hi. Welcome to my home. Would you like me to show you around?" I asked, holding out my arms. I loved this house. I had made it mine, and while I might be a little more anal-retentive than some of my friends, I could relax here. And I did not want my parents and my cousin to jeopardize the sanctity of what I had built here.

Only it didn't seem as if I had a choice.

"We are here now," my father began, "and we don't need to see your home. But there are a few things we need to discuss."

"Oh?" I asked, confused.

"It's about Grandma Sharon," Roland answered.

My heart twisted, and I took a step forward, my hand outstretched. "Is she okay? We have our scheduled call tomorrow, but I haven't heard anything from her this week. We've both been busy. She always sends cat memes, but it's been...I guess it's been longer than usual." Worry filled me, and I put my hands in front of myself, clasping them together.

"Your grandmother passed," my mother said, waving her hand in the air as if it weren't her mother who died.

I staggered back, placing my hand on my chest. "What? Grandma Sharon is dead?" I asked, tears filling my eyes. "When? And you came here to tell me in person? What happened?"

"It was last week." My mother fixed her hair even though not a strand was out of place. "She fell asleep and didn't wake up. The funeral was two days ago."

Shock slid through me, and I took another step back, running into the armchair in the sitting room. I sank onto its cushions, trying to catch my breath. Grandma Sharon had been the one person in my family who always understood me. She had bought me my first paint set, had taught me how to work with watercolors and oils, and had taken me to different art classes when my mother said it was useless. She had been the one to show me who I could be if I let myself. She helped me apply to out-of-state colleges when my parents were opposed. She tried to help me find my way when I came back from Colorado brokenhearted. We had drifted apart slightly when I moved back here, needing space from my family and wanting to be near Hazel. But we talked weekly.

"How could you not tell me? Grandma Sharon is dead? And you already had the funeral? Without me?"

"There's no need to be dramatic," my father chided. "There's nothing you can do about it. There was a small ceremony with family."

"*I'm* family," I growled.

"Watch your tone," my mother snapped.

"No, this is my home. We're under my roof. I can say whatever the hell I want to. I can yell if I want. You barged into my home without saying you were coming, and now you're telling me my grandmother is dead? And acting as if you don't care?"

"Of course, I care, Myra," my mother said. "She was my mother. But there's nothing I can do. She's dead. And you need to stop acting like a petulant child. You're the one who left us. You're the one who came back to this godforsaken state to be with the mountain people or whatever the hell it is you love here. You left us. You decided to cut the ties. And I'm sorry if we couldn't bow to your precious schedule."

"How the hell could I bow to *your* schedule when I didn't know the funeral was going to happen?" I asked, pain slapping me in the face. "You didn't even call to tell me. And yet you flew out here? I don't understand."

"Your grandmother's lawyer set up the reading of the will here." My mother's voice was crisp. I simply sat there as my cousin glared, and my parents looked annoyed to be in the same room with me. They stood, hovering, and I felt walled off and as if I were two steps behind. I didn't know what to do.

"The will," I whispered. "This is all about money?"

My father snarled. "Life is about money, Myra. My mother-in-law set up the reading of her will to be in this state for some reason, even though she resided in California for forty years."

"But she was from here originally," I whispered. She had been a huge part of why I moved to Colorado.

"Why are you here, truly?" I asked, too tired to deal with my emotions. Everything hurt, and I wanted to be able to allow myself to feel that, but I couldn't do that while they were watching. I had never been able to, and now, it was only worse.

"The reading of the will is next week. We are staying in downtown Denver. We'll give you our information. You need to be at the will reading since you are listed as a beneficiary. You are required to be there."

"Okay," I said. "Just give me the information, and I will see you there. I don't know why you didn't tell me when it happened."

"Not everything is about you, Myra," my mother spat.

"I see," I whispered.

"It's okay, cuz." Roland smiled. "I didn't know you didn't know about Grandma, but you know she loved you the most. She'll take care of you."

I looked over at Roland, wondering what he expected me to say. We had never gotten along, but he had never been cruel to me like some of my other cousins had. He was nothing but a rich boy who worked for his dad and liked the money that came from his mother—my mother's sister. He was probably waiting on a large inheritance from Grandmother to help fulfill his next phase of life. I didn't care. I had money from the other side of the family. And from work. What I wanted was my grandmother. And here I was, not even allowed to grieve. Not yet, at least.

"Hey, the door was open, are you okay?"

I turned, nearly falling out of my chair at the sound of Nate's voice. He walked in, his eyes wide as he looked at me. And then they narrowed into slits as my parents turned as one to face him.

"Nathan," my mother bit out.

I looked between them, confused. "Wait, you know each other?" I asked.

"Of course, we know each other," Nate said. "They're the ones that showed me the photos of you cheating on me."

I looked at him, and my world tilted on its axis as I turned to my parents and finally understood.

"What the hell?" I asked.

Though I was afraid I already knew the answer.

Chapter 7

Nate

I STOOD IN MYRA'S SITTING ROOM, WONDERING IF I'D somehow crossed a portal into the past. One of the worst moments of my life was now staring back at me in full force.

Her parents might look slightly older—not much, if I were honest—but they had the same expression they'd had the last time I saw them.

Disappointment.

Anger.

Pity.

And, once again, I didn't know which of the three

were for me and what was for Myra. Probably a mix of all of them.

Myra looked at her parents and I had a feeling I'd fucked up. Not now. Not in this moment. But years ago. I looked between them and I knew I'd been decided, and I'd made the biggest mistake of my life. A colossal misstep that I'd never be able to come back from.

"What the hell?" Myra asked, her hand shaking at her sides.

"Myra, what did I say about that tone?" her mother snapped. I took two striding steps forward to stand at Myra's side. We may have been on opposite sides of many encounters recently. But right now, I was on her side. I didn't know why. I didn't know what would happen next, but something was going on. What I did know was that I did not want to be in the dark.

"I told you before, this is my home. How do you know Nate?"

"It was a long time ago, Myra," her father said offhandedly, waving off the entire situation as if he hadn't had a hand in breaking Myra and me up.

"No, it's happening right now. *How* do you know Nathan?"

"We met with him to make sure the family got what it needed."

My stomach churned, and I felt as if the world had crashed down around me. I couldn't breathe.

"Those photos were fake, weren't they?" I asked, my mouth dry.

"Photos? What photos?" Myra whispered, her face pale as I looked over at her.

"Jesus Christ." I gasped.

"Stop being so overdramatic," her father snapped. "Of course, we knew about the marriage. You two were far too young to get married. And who is this man? A Brady? No, Myra. You had to go off and marry someone so beneath your station that no one had ever fucking heard of him," her father shouted.

"What did you do?" Myra asked, her voice steady.

Far stronger than I felt.

I saw the younger man in the room smirk for just a second before his face smoothed to a carefully neutral expression.

I didn't know who the asshole was, but now he was a witness to whatever travesty was happening, and I honestly wanted to punch his smarmy little face.

"The photos that you showed me of Myra with her boyfriend. Those were fake, weren't they?" I asked, trying to keep my voice calm.

"Again, what photos?" Myra whispered. "You showed him pictures of Alexander and me?" Myra asked. "How could you do that? What did you…? *Why* would you think that's okay? Where did you get them? You *faked* photos?"

Her mother sighed, pinched the bridge of her nose, and gestured around the room. "It seems we have a lot to talk about. And I'm not going to stand here without a drink in my hand. Since you never were good at making me a martini, I guess we're going to sit and hash this out, and then I'm going to go and get a drink."

"No, you're going to explain what the fuck is going on. Right now," I growled, trying to keep my voice smooth—it wasn't happening.

"You don't get to use those words with me," her father said coolly.

Myra snarled. "I will deal with Nate later, but right now, he's allowed to say whatever the fuck he wants to say."

"Apparently, we're all going to curse now," her mother grumbled, sighing before draping herself dramatically in an armchair.

"You were too young to get married," her father began. "You were eighteen years old, Myra. You had no right to go behind our backs and marry this white trash piece of shit with no future."

"You're going to want to be very careful about how you speak to me and how you speak to your daughter."

"Are you threatening me?" her father asked, his eyes narrowed.

"I should be the one threatening you," Myra shot back. "I was eighteen years old, as you said. An adult. You had no right to stand in my way."

"You were a *child*." Her mother sighed. "You went off to Vegas and married a little boy who didn't know what he wanted."

"You're going to want to stop talking about me in that way," I said, my voice deceptively calm and casual.

"And what are you going to do about it?" her father asked.

I took a breath. "I want answers, and then you're going to leave."

I looked over at Myra, knowing that I needed to say something to her. She deserved so much more than what I had given her.

I was trying to keep up.

She hadn't cheated on me.

I had lost the best thing in my life because I was a fucking idiot and didn't question what I was told.

I'd wanted to latch onto whatever truth I was dealt, and I had ruined everything.

There was no way she would ever forgive me.

I hadn't given her a chance to explain.

I had worked hard for so many years, trying to

decide if I could ever forgive her. And in the end, I was the one who needed forgiveness.

Dear God, she should hate me forever.

No wonder I felt as if she already did.

Her mother waved her hand. "You came out here on my mother's whim."

"The mother you never told me died." Myra's voice broke.

I frowned but didn't interrupt. Not yet.

"Again with the hysterics, Myra? For the love of God, just stop it. You were eighteen. You didn't know what you were doing."

"I knew what I was doing and thinking, Mother. I loved him."

"And now you sound like a Disney princess flailing about," her father said, pacing the room.

"You showed my husband doctored photographs?"

"And he easily believed them," her mother added. "What does that tell you?"

I opened my mouth to say something, but Myra held up a hand. "That's something the two of us will deal with later."

"Oh, yes, I'm sure you will," the other man in the room remarked.

"Stay out of this, Roland. I don't even know why you're here," Myra snapped.

"I'm a neutral party."

"Did you know about this?" Myra said. "Did you know what my parents did?"

"Honestly, I didn't even know you had gotten married. So you're a divorcee and not a spinster? Interesting. It only makes sense why you'd move out to the boonies. Surprised you don't have a dozen cats and haven't taken up knitting. Still working on your little paintings, cuz?"

I reached out and touched the small of Myra's back. She jolted and looked over her shoulder at me. I was afraid she might reach out and punch the smug little prick. Since I wanted to do exactly that, I wouldn't have blamed her, but it wouldn't get us anywhere.

"Let me get this straight…" Myra began, taking a deep breath. I lowered my hand.

I felt the loss immediately, and yet I didn't know what I was supposed to think or feel.

She hadn't cheated on me. And I hadn't believed her. I had pushed her out and hurt her. I'd hurt her so much, I couldn't understand why I had let myself believe the horrible things her parents led me to believe.

The evidence had been right there, yes, and yet…I should have questioned it. But I hadn't.

"You believed that you could change my life. That you could make my decisions for me," Myra continued.

"We were paying for your college. We let you come out here for a year to see what it was like seeing as my mother talked about it so often. And yet, you were doing nothing with your life. You weren't maintaining the GPA that we required of you."

"You paid a small percentage. I got scholarships for the rest. I'd have paid for it all myself if I had to. If I'd known. And I had a 4.0," she said.

"Yes, but in the easy classes. The harder ones were coming up, and you were not striving to do your best. You were getting distracted by this boy." Her father sighed, waving his hand in my direction.

"I was not distracted." Myra put her hands over her face and let out a deep breath. I wanted to reach out and touch her, tell her that everything was okay. But I didn't believe that. I didn't know what the hell was going on. I could barely keep up with my feelings, let alone know how to help her.

"We did what was best for you," her father snapped.

"So, you what? Hired someone to manipulate a photo? I know you're not that good with Photoshop."

Her father snorted. "We did what we had to do. You looked a lot like the woman your ex was seeing at the time, and he was all too happy to take photos for a little monetary enticement. He added the bracelet that you wore to ensure that your so-called husband believed what he saw."

Her dad went on about her ex and how they would have been perfect for each other, and yet I couldn't quite believe what I was hearing.

"If her ex was so perfect for her, then why did he take the money? Sounds like a weak ass loser to me," I said, sounding like I had when I first met Myra, not like the man I was now. I felt so lost.

"Weak?" Her mother laughed. "You're the one who believed a simple photo. You were so easy to convince that our daughter was cheating on you. You let us take her away without a fight. What kind of man are you?"

"You need to go," Myra said after a moment, her voice calm. *Too* calm.

"Yes, Nathan, you should go." Her mother raised her chin.

"No, he can stay."

"You're going back to him?" her father asked incredulously.

"Please don't, that's so cliché." Her cousin rolled his eyes.

"It is none of your concern what I do in this home or this state or this world. You need to go. Now. I will see you at the lawyer's office. But I am done with this. I am done with you. You thought you could control me?

Fuck you. You never could. All you did was ruin everything. Take away all that I've ever wanted. Over and over again. You took my happiness, my future. You took my chance to say goodbye to my grandmother. To Nate. You took everything. All because you thought you knew best. I came out here because I know better. I know what I need. And it's not you."

"I do wish you would stop with all the melodramatics." Her mother sighed, sounding far more melodramatic to me.

She stood up, brushed off her already impeccably clean suit, then picked up a bag and walked away without another word. Her father glared at me and then pushed past me.

Her cousin simply smirked. "Are you sure the photos weren't of you? You always were a whore."

I took a step forward, but before I could reach out and punch the guy, her cousin staggered back, Myra having slapped him hard across the face. She went at him again, and I looped an arm around her waist, pulling her back.

"He looks like the kind of man who will sue," I whispered into her ear, and she froze against me, her soft curves molding to the hardness of my chest.

"Go," she said through gritted teeth. The other man rubbed his jaw, smirked again, and then strode out. He slammed the front door, and I stood there,

Myra in my arms. And then I realized that I needed to let her go.

I didn't want to.

"Please take your hands off me."

I released her quickly and took a step back. "I'm sorry."

She turned slowly. "Sorry for what? Touching me? Not letting me hit him again? Or for believing that I could be the person my parents led you to believe I was?"

"I... I don't know what to say, Myra."

My heart thudded in my ears, and everything came back to me.

"I thought... If you would have seen the photos…"

"But I didn't see them. You pushed me out without even letting me speak. You believed my parents."

"I believed what I thought was evidence."

"So, you're a detective now?"

Tears streamed down her face, and I swallowed hard, not knowing what to say.

"I... I didn't... I didn't know what to believe. I saw the bracelet, and everything I thought about you got twisted."

"Because you thought I was capable of that kind of deception."

I shook my head. "Because I thought you were

always so much better than me. That I didn't deserve you."

"So you pushed me away?" she shouted.

"I thought you could do better, and believed you had. So, yes, I was hurt. I pushed you away. I thought you had cheated on me and I said some horrible things. And I hated you. But I was so fucking wrong. I see that now. And I'm never going to be able to take that back. I'm so sorry, Myra.

"Sorry doesn't help," she whispered.

"I know."

"You had the evidence they provided, yet you never believed me. No wonder you didn't want to forgive me, even though I wasn't the one who did anything."

"Myra—" I began.

"No. I think you need to go, too. Because I need to break down, and you can't be here for that. You broke me once before, Nathan. I won't let you do it again."

"I understand." I put my hands into my pockets and let out a breath. "I need to think about everything that just happened. As you do. I want you to know that I'm going to do everything in my power to try and make amends or something. I'm so fucking sorry, Myra."

"I don't know if I care," she said, then she paused. "I think I need to tell the girls."

I swallowed hard. "I think you do. You need to talk to someone, and I know it can't be me."

"No, Nathan. I don't think it can ever be you."

The metaphorical knife twisted in my chest, but I deserved it. I looked at her then, at the tears on her cheeks, at the fact that she looked as if she couldn't breathe.

And I walked away.

Again.

Chapter 8

Myra

Four days later, I still wasn't sure that I was making the right decision. It was the only choice I could make, but lack of sleep and too much caffeine had sent me into overdrive with poor decision-making skills. I was usually better than this, but then again, maybe I wasn't. If I had been good at making the correct choices, at laying out my options and doing what I needed to do, I wouldn't be in this situation. But now, here I was, in my car on my way to Hazel's to tell my friends that I had been keeping a dramatic secret from them for as long as I had known them. And in Hazel's case, that was quite a long time.

Not only was it a deep secret that could be construed as a lie in some cases, but it also involved someone we all knew, and had a layered history that I was only now becoming aware of. I wouldn't be surprised if my friends hated me forever given what they were about to learn, but I would find a way to make everything right.

I swallowed hard and gripped the steering wheel. "Or, they'll drop everything and help me make things better, and I'll run away because I have no idea what the hell I'm doing." I sighed. Great, now I was talking to myself and trying to lie and say that everything was fine when it clearly wasn't.

I sat at the stop sign two blocks from Hazel's house and knew I needed to get this over with. The sooner I did it, the better for everybody. It didn't make it any easier, though. I looked both ways and made my way across the intersection. A horn blared, and I slammed on my brakes, skidding as a passing car nearly hit me. It must have run the stop sign, and my heart raced, my palms going clammy, my ears ringing.

"Breathe, breathe. You're fine."

I pulled over to the side of the road and looked for the other car, only I didn't see it. I vaguely remembered seeing a dark vehicle out of the corner of my eye, but I couldn't remember what make or model it was or exactly what had happened. Since I hadn't hit them and they hadn't hit me, I guessed it didn't matter in the end.

The other vehicle had been inches from me. If I hadn't slammed on my brakes, something I probably shouldn't have done in the first place, I could've been hit. And considering that it had been coming at my driver's side door, I probably would've died. Even with me going twenty miles an hour. The person in the other car had definitely been speeding.

I swallowed hard, bile filling my throat.

"Oh my God," I said, my hands shaking. "This isn't a sign. It totally isn't a sign."

I took another deep breath, trying to calm myself. The guy had just run a stop sign. The whole thing had only scared me a bit. But whoever it was had driven away, seemingly not caring at all, even though it had been their fault. Would they have even stopped if they had hit me?

If they had been forced to stop because of the collision, sure. Still, it freaked me out. I didn't like the idea that I had nearly died, and no one was around to witness it.

I shook my head, pushing those thoughts from my brain. Just because I was nervous about what was about to happen didn't mean I had to be so melancholic. I had people who cared about me. Friends. Family I had made. Simply because most of my relatives seemed to be horrible didn't mean that I didn't have people who cared for and about me.

And I was going to see three of them now. I really hoped my friends *continued* to care about me once they learned my secret.

I pulled out onto the road again, made another turn, and parked in front of Hazel's home. The girls were already here. I was the last to arrive, something I had done on purpose. Not to make an entrance as Paris might have jokingly accused, but because I needed time to plan.

I reached over to the passenger side seat and picked up my purse and the two bottles of wine that thankfully hadn't moved since I had secured them tightly. If I hadn't, they would have ended up splattered all over my dashboard when I slammed on my brakes. I always protected my wine, even if it was only a joke between my friends. But now I could only think about what else could have been smashed if that car had actually hit me.

I shook my head, telling myself that I was only focusing on that as a distraction from what I needed to tell my friends. I got out of the car and made my way to Hazel's front stoop. She opened the door before I even had a chance to reach the front step and smiled at me.

I only hoped she would continue smiling once she heard the truth.

"Hey there. I was about to send out the cavalry because you weren't here yet." I held up the bottle of wine.

"Are you sure you weren't missing our day wine?" I asked, keeping my tone light.

"That too." She smiled again, then hugged me tightly and took the bottles. As she pulled away, her eyes narrowed on my face. "What happened?"

I opened my mouth to say something and then promptly burst into tears.

I didn't know who was more shocked, Hazel or me. She pulled me into the house, closing the door tightly behind me.

"Girls. We need you."

I shook her off, wiping my face. "I'm fine. I don't know what came over me."

"Something sure did," Paris said. And then I was in her hold, her strong little arms hugging me tightly. I sobbed even harder. Dakota's soft arms were around me then, the same as Hazel's. The three of them stood around me, cocooning me in a shelter of love and support as I let everything out.

I hadn't even told them anything yet, and I was

already breaking. What would happen when I finally said the words?

I leaned into my friends, sank into the comforting embrace I wasn't even sure I deserved, and was finally able to breathe again. I had been holding in so much over the years, not to mention what I had been doing for the past few days.

Finally, I pulled away slightly, and they let me have some space, worry still in each of their gazes. My friends were so different, so much their own people, but their masks were all identical now. Worry for me. And, again, I wasn't sure I deserved it.

"I know you called us because you wanted to talk to us," Paris began. "But if it's so bad, do you need a moment?" she asked, and I shook my head.

"No, I think I need to go over it now. All at once."

"Do you want to tell us exactly why you're so pale first?" Hazel asked, her voice careful. Oh, so careful.

I swallowed hard. "I'm pale because I almost got into an accident on my way over here."

"Are you okay?" Dakota asked, sounding aghast. She reached out and cupped my cheek. "What happened?"

I explained about the stop sign, and Paris frowned. "That's a pretty well-known intersection. Teenagers sometimes miss it," she explained.

Hazel bit her lip. “I’m so sorry that happened. Do you need to sit down?”

I shook my head. “I think I need to stand for this.” I swallowed hard again. “Perhaps you should be sitting, though,” I said softly.

“We can do that.” Dakota met my gaze. “But first, are you sure you don’t need to sit?”

“Please, sit. And then I’ll go over everything.”

“I have a feeling we may need wine,” Paris said, taking the bottles from Hazel’s hands as she went off to the kitchen. Dakota tugged at my hand and pulled me into the living room. They had set out deviled eggs and a few other crudités and appetizers. Dakota had gone all out, and I knew Hazel had helped. However, Dakota was the chef among us, even though she called herself a home baker.

I wanted nothing. I knew that anything I ate would likely taste like sawdust, and it would be a disservice to Dakota’s talents.

Hazel came back in with the open wine bottle, and that’s when I noticed that there were already wine glasses and water on the table.

“Thank you for bringing it over in an insulated sack because Rosé All Day needs to be chilled,” Paris said, pouring glasses for us. I noticed that she gave me the largest one, and I didn’t blame her.

I had no idea what I looked like to them, but I

knew it wasn't the composed Myra I had tried so hard to be for so long. We clinked glasses, and I took a large gulp.

"Okay, now, tell us what's on your mind," Paris ordered.

I looked down at the rosé in my glass, studying the pink liquid, wondering if I could chug it and forget about why I was here in the first place. The other women gazed at me, all three of them thankfully sitting down. I stood, ready to pace if needed. No, I couldn't simply drink my worries away. I had to tell them everything.

"I don't know where to begin," I whispered.

"Timelines usually work," Paris said.

"Hush," Hazel admonished, and Paris shrugged. I knew she was trying to help, and I was grateful, but I needed to tell them everything. And to do so, I had to throw my carefully planned speech out the window.

"My parents came here four days ago."

Hazel's eyes widened. "They were here? I didn't even know they knew where you lived." That made me snort, while Paris and Dakota frowned at each other.

"We do not get along. Shocking, I know." None of us really got along with our parents, so I wasn't the outcast.

"I moved away when things went beyond annoying

and began to get unbearable, and I decided to come out here with Hazel, to a place I loved before."

"I remember you saying you went to college in Colorado for a year," Dakota added.

"I did. I loved this area because it was my grandmother's home before she met my grandfather and moved to California." My voice cracked, and Hazel set down her glass.

"Is your grandmother okay?" Hazel asked. She had met Grandma Sharon a few times when we were in California, and once here when Grandma came to visit.

I shook my head, my eyes filling with tears. Hazel was up in an instant, hugging me tightly, but I had to push her away. "I won't be able to finish if you're hugging me. I'm so sorry."

Hazel wiped my cheeks and then nodded; her eyes now filled with tears.

"Of course. What happened?" she asked.

I looked at my wine, took another sip, and then set it down. I hadn't eaten anything all day, and this would likely go right to my head if I wasn't careful. "My parents came here with my cousin Roland to tell me that Grandma passed."

"That asshole came with them?" Hazel asked and then held out her hand. "Sorry. But I hate your cousin."

"I hate him, too. But yes, he was here." I paused. "My grandmother had been dead for over a week. *A week*," I repeated. "They already had the funeral. And they didn't tell me. I didn't even know that she was gone." I swallowed hard.

"I was planning to call her for our normal call. But I'd been so in my head, I hadn't even realized it had been a while since I'd gotten an email or update. A week. She never let that much time pass. My family didn't tell me anything, you guys. My parents and Roland and the others basically hid her death from me."

"Those fuckers," Paris snapped.

"I can't believe they would do that," Dakota said. "I mean, I don't know them, so this might be right in their wheelhouse, but that's so cruel. I can see from the way you're grieving that you loved your grandmother."

"I did. *I do*. I don't know what the right tense is supposed to be. I haven't even had a chance to grieve. They came here because I'm supposed to meet with the lawyer soon about the will. It's all about money to them. It always has been. They didn't even have the decency to call or anything to tell me that my grandmother was dead. My mother's mother is dead, and they didn't tell me anything until well after the fact. They clearly washed their hands of me after I finally left their precious home and decided that I needed to be my own person. Which is fine. But they decided that I didn't get to have anything to do with the family. They cut me out. And while I appreciate not having to deal with them, they took something precious from me, and I'm never going to forgive them."

"I don't blame you," Dakota said softly.

"That's not the only thing I won't forgive them for," I whispered and then looked over at Hazel. "There's something I need to tell all of you. Something that you may hate me for. But I need you to listen while I explain. And I need you to not shove me out of the house and hate me, at least until I finish. Can you promise to do that?" I asked.

"You're worrying me."

I looked at Paris. "I know. And I'm sorry. I'll likely deserve everything you'll probably shove at me later, but if I don't get it out now, and all at once, I'll never be able to."

"Tell us," Hazel said, her voice a little cold.

I took a deep breath, and then I told them. "Nate is my ex-husband," I blurted.

"Are you fucking kidding me?" Paris asked.

"Paris, I'm sure she's kidding. Right?" Dakota asked.

Hazel looked at me in silence, her eyes narrowed.

"When I moved to Colorado for college, Nate and I met, and we fell in love. Somehow, we got it into our brains that we should get married. And that's what we did when we were in Vegas for spring break."

They were silent for a moment, and my pulse raced. What would happen if they pushed me away? What would I say? What could I do? I couldn't imagine my life without them in it, and yet, I knew I wouldn't be able to blame these wonderful women if they never wanted to see me again.

Dakota let out a breath. "You were married. To our Nate. And you never told us?"

I shook my head, my hands shaking. "No. I didn't. But yes, we were married. We thought it was us against the world, but it turned out that it wasn't."

"And that's why you hate each other so much," Dakota whispered.

"Maybe. As it turns out, it was all a complete misunderstanding," I said dryly.

"That you were married?" Paris asked snidely.

"No, we went into that with our heads full of promise and love and stupidity. My parents made sure they broke us up, though."

Silence filled the room as the others tried to keep up. I felt like I was drowning.

"They wouldn't have liked Nate," Hazel added.

"No, they wouldn't," I replied. "Apparently, they found out. My family always had people watching me. They had enough money and could do anything. And they did. They found out I married Nate, and they doctored photos to show that I was cheating on him with my ex-boyfriend. And Nathan believed them."

"You call him Nathan," Dakota whispered.

"He believed you cheated?" Paris asked. "What a fucking asshole."

"You were married," Hazel said again.

I shook my head and then sat down on the ottoman in front of the table. "Yes. I call him Nathan. It was a thing between us, and sometimes it comes out. And yes, he believed them, but he had proof—or so he thought. I don't know who would blame him. And, yes…we were married."

I looked at the others, and they stared. I could see them thinking hard and trying to piece everything together, and I knew I needed to keep going. "It all came out when Nathan came to the house to talk to me. We've been trying for a truce, you see. I hated him because he never trusted me, and he hated me because he thought I cheated. Anyway, he came to the house the other day when my parents were there, and the truth came out. Nate and I haven't talked since. We will, though I don't know what'll come of it. But I told him I needed to tell you. And he's telling his family now."

"Oh my God," Hazel muttered. "His brothers are going to hate this."

"It all started off wrong," I continued. "When you introduced me to him, I didn't know how to tell you that we already knew each other. In so many ways." I laughed hollowly. "How was I supposed to tell you that I had married the person I thought was the love of my life, and that it had turned out to be a moment that shattered me into a million pieces?"

"We're your best friends, you should've told us," Dakota said, and my heart broke once more. "But we understand about secrets. I get why you couldn't tell us before we met him. But why keep up with the lie afterwards?"

I looked down at my hands, frowning. "It snow-balled, I guess." I shrugged and looked up at Hazel. "I didn't know you would fall for Cross. I didn't know that his family and the family that I made would intertwine so much. But when everything happened, it became this taboo thing where I couldn't speak the words that I needed to, and he couldn't either. We just hid the secrets because we were afraid of the outcome, and now there's no going back. I'm so sorry. I'm sorry I lied —I'm sorry *we* lied. I hope you can forgive me. Because I'm breaking inside over many things right now, and I don't know what I'll do if you guys walk away from me."

They were silent for a moment, and I was afraid that this was it. Would they tell me to leave, and make me lose everything? I'd lost the one person in my birth family that I loved more than anything, I had lost Nathan years ago, and now, I was afraid I would lose the family of my heart, too.

Hazel stood up first, and I rose as well, ready to leave if I needed to. But then she opened her arms and pulled me close, and the tears fell again.

"I'm so sorry you were afraid that we would walk away. We've all made mistakes, and now have to deal with the consequences," Hazel said. "And the consequences mean that we're going to be all growly with you, but we still love you."

Dakota leaned forward. "You've been through so much. All of us have. We don't toss out our family because of a single mistake."

I shook, my tears still falling. "It's more than a single mistake," I countered.

"It's like you *want* to get rid of us," Paris teased.

"I have no idea what I'm doing. I'm trying not to freak out, but I am. Everything that I thought was the truth is a lie. My parents deliberately pushed Nate away from me. And I loved him, you guys. I loved him more than anything. I thought we were going to be each other's forevers. As it turns out, he thought the worst of me. And I don't know how to get past that. And now, he's constantly in my life, and in yours, and I can't walk away. Add that to the fact that I still don't know what to think about losing my grandmother and not being able to say goodbye, and the idea that Nathan and I still have to talk… It's so much. I need you guys. Help me figure this out. Please."

"You're our sister," Hazel said simply. "We're always with you. And now, we're going to help you figure out what to do."

The tears streamed harder, and I fell into my girls. "I don't know what I'm going to do," I whispered.

Hazel let out a breath. "But you don't need to figure it out right now. At this moment, you're going to eat to soak up some of that wine, and then you're going to tell us exactly what happened. Slowly. And in detail. And then we'll decide if we have to kick Nate's ass or not."

I laughed and held them each close, marveling at how lucky I was, even after making so many mistakes. But in the end, I knew it wouldn't be their decisions that brought me to the next step. I needed to take that alone.

But I had no idea where to begin.

Chapter 9

Nate

"Okay, are you going to tell us why you gathered us here today?" Cross asked as he picked up a chip and dipped it into the sour cream and onion dip that Arden had made.

I rubbed my temples and nodded. "Yes, soon. I figured we should eat first." I paused, my stomach turning. "Or maybe we should skip eating and I'll just get this over with."

Prior walked into the dining room, ribs and wings on a platter in front of him before he set them down on the table next to the salads we had set out earlier.

He gave me a curious look, and I shook my head, trying to collect my thoughts.

I ran my hand over my face as Macon walked in, his phone in his grip. "Joshua is hanging with his friends tonight. He was texting me photos of a frog they found." He showed off his phone, and Arden took it, grinning.

My puppy, Daisy, Arden's dog, Jasper, and the two puppies Macon had adopted were around our feet, trying to get food but well-behaved enough not to jump on the table to grab a bite for themselves. Only Jasper could reach easily, but Arden's Husky was well-trained and doing his best to look regal and proper, showing the younger pups exactly how to act when it came to human food. I didn't feed Daisy scraps, but she whined sometimes for treats. Hopefully, being around Jasper would help her not do that anymore.

Arden sighed. "Aw, that boy is so cute."

"Yeah, he is," Macon said, flashing her a dopey smile.

If Myra and I had made it and hadn't walked away from each other, would we have a child around Joshua's age? I wondered why the thought of that didn't fill me with trepidation. Instead, all I felt was a dull ache. Grief for what was lost and would never be found again.

We had lost our chance. Hadn't we? The fact that I

didn't have a concrete answer to that worried me. But before I could talk with Myra and find a way to grovel and tell her exactly how sorry I was, I had to open up to my family.

And that was far easier said than done.

Cross cleared his throat. "Okay, let's get some food in us before Nate tells us why he gathered us here today."

I met Arden's gaze, and her eyes widened.

She knew exactly why we were here, even if I hadn't told her ahead of time. I probably should have warned her, but I'd been so deep in my head, as well as focused on my deadline, that I had invited everybody over to Arden's for dinner, and nobody had said a word about it. We all did that. Arden and Liam had the best house. Now that we were here, we would have our family meeting, and hopefully, they wouldn't disown me by the end of it. Unfortunately, I'd been so focused on what to say, even if I had come up with nothing, that I hadn't told Arden ahead of time.

But now she knew. She must.

Everybody ate ribs and salad and beans as I picked at my food, and Arden gave me a weird look.

"Okay, you need to get on with it," Prior said, setting his plate down as he looked over his shoulder. I followed his gaze to where the dogs were behind a gate, all looking innocent but clearly craving ribs.

We were still working on training, and that meant even Jasper wasn't allowed near us during mealtimes. I hated that we had to do it, but it was better for everybody. Soon, the puppies would be big enough, and we wouldn't have to worry. But for now, they had to be separated. Even though all I wanted to do was feed them ribs and pretend that I hadn't fucked up my life —numerous times.

"Hey. Come on, talk to us," Cross ordered.

I set my uneaten plate on the table and put my hands over my face. "I fucked up."

"Normally, I'd ask if you got someone pregnant, but I don't think you've been seeing anybody recently." Cross paused. "Except for Myra."

My gaze shot to his. "Myra's not pregnant," I said quickly. She hadn't been when we were together, either.

"You need to tell them, Nate," Arden said softly.

Everyone's gaze moved to her.

"You know why we're here?" Macon asked.

"Yes, I do. And I know you're probably going to yell at me but give us a moment." Arden raised her chin. "Be kind and let him speak. We'll deal with what happens next."

I sighed, knowing this wasn't going to be easy.

"What is she talking about?" Cross asked, looking at me.

"Myra is my ex-wife…" I began again.

Prior choked on his beer and then began laughing. "Really? That's what you're going with? Okay. Whatever you say."

Macon blinked at me before shaking his head. "Did you lose all your money gambling or something? Is it the concussion? Because it's not that."

Cross looked between Arden and me and then let out a curse under his breath. "I think you're going to need to explain. Slowly."

I looked up at my big brother and nodded. My other brothers quieted, their eyes now comically wide.

"Jesus Christ, you're serious," Prior said.

"When did you have time to get married to Myra? And how the hell did you already get a divorce? And how didn't we know? It's not like we've known her for long."

I sighed at Macon's words but then began. "Myra went to my college for a little bit. We met then and fell in love. We got married over spring break." I explained about the coffee and our relationship and how we planned to tell everyone when we got back but wanted to keep it to ourselves for a bit.

In retrospect, it was idiotic. And we were fooling ourselves thinking that we could ever make it work without talking to our families. But we had been young, stupid, and had liked the secret at the time.

"And you knew?" Prior asked, turning towards Arden. She nodded.

"He's my twin. Of course, I knew." She paused. "And I caught Myra with her engagement ring."

"Holy shit," Macon whispered.

"But that's not even the worst part," I added.

"The fact that you got married and divorced without telling us isn't the worst part? You're going to need to explain," Cross said.

"I fucked up."

"Did you cheat on her?" Macon growled.

I shook my head. "Maybe it would have been easier if I had."

The others cursed, and I pressed my lips together, trying to hold back the pain and the anger. All the things that had been whirling inside me for years.

"You never told me why," Arden said. "You only said it didn't work out, and then you pushed me away. You finished school, and then the accident happened, and I did my best to ignore it all. But you need to tell us more. Please, Nate. Talk to us."

I nodded at my twin's words and told them about Myra's parents, and the pictures, and the fact that I had pushed her away. I told them how I now knew I had been wrong—oh so fucking wrong. And, throughout the story, they all stayed silent.

I was grateful for that.

I started to pace, as did Prior. Macon sat stoically, as did Cross. Arden wiped a tear from her face, and I hated that she felt bad about any of it.

"I should have told you. Long before this. But it hurt so fucking much. I felt as if I had tried to make my first adult decision and messed up to the point where I couldn't even trust myself. I was hurt, angry, and I pushed everyone away because of it. And then, like Arden said, by the time I came out of my stupor, the accident happened, and we had a whole other slew of things to worry about."

"We always have things when it comes to us," Cross said but held up his hand when I tried to explain. "But, honestly, I don't blame you for not telling us." I blinked at him, surprised.

"You don't?" Prior asked.

"No. We have all had our heads up our asses at one time or another. You know he would have told us eventually if things had worked out. But they didn't. And, yes, you fucked up. I don't know how I feel about the idea that you had this whole secret that you kept from us. But how were you supposed to bring it up?"

"I don't know. I'm not doing a very decent job of it *now*."

"You're doing better than you give yourself credit for," Macon said softly. "I don't know what I would have done if I'd found out the person I loved cheated on me. I can see why you wanted to hide it. But now that you know it was a lie, what are you going to do about it?" Macon asked.

"That's my question, too," Arden added. "Myra's in our lives, Nate. She's always going to be there. And you're our brother. You're not going anywhere. So, what are you going to do?" she asked.

"I have no idea. I don't know what I'm supposed to do."

"Did you apologize?" Cross asked.

"I tried, but we were also trying to push her parents out and deal with her fucking cousin at the same time."

"They sound like horrible people," Prior said.

"They are. Only I didn't realize how evil they were until it was too late."

Arden shook her head. "You need to apologize again."

"I know," I agreed.

"No, we need you to do the best groveling you can. You can talk to Liam and the guys in this room. Because I know they've all groveled."

"Hey," Prior said, acting affronted.

"It's the truth." Arden raised a brow.

Prior shrugged. "Okay, true."

Arden continued. "You also need to apologize more than once and show her that you're sorry. Don't use only your words."

"You're speaking as if I want her back and not just apologizing to pay penance for the hell I put her through."

"Don't you?" she asked.

"No. I've never let myself think like that anyway. I'm not the person I was before. And she's not the woman she was. I don't know if I want to get past what happened and what we went through. Or if we even can."

Arden shook her head. "You'll never know until you get over the first hurdle of trying to find forgiveness. You spent so long not being able to forgive her. I can tell. Now it's her turn to find some semblance of forgiveness for you."

"I don't think I deserve it."

"And that's the first step," my twin agreed. "Acceptance. Now, do what you can. Because she's a good person. Her parents tried to ruin everything, but you're both complicit in what happened after and for not speaking to each other."

"What am I supposed to do if she doesn't forgive me?" I asked. "Because I need her to know that I'm sorry. I know I hurt her. I understand that."

"Then tell her that. Show her. And once you get to the other side, figure out what you're going to do. Because you're going to be in each other's lives. What roles you play is up to you. But mostly, it's up to her."

I swallowed hard and looked at my family, knowing that they were right. Sadly, I had no idea what I was going to do about it. My brothers tried to help and attempted to give me pointers, but they were as lost as I was.

I'd have to figure this out on my own.

I packed up Daisy in her little car seat and took a to-go container of my dinner since I hadn't eaten anything. I was too worried about what they were going to say. I got in the car and on the road, thinking that had gone better than expected. Honestly, I had been afraid they might hit me for lying to them for so long.

If anything, they seemed angrier at her parents than me, and I agreed with them. I wanted to lash out at her mom and dad for what they did, too. Yes, they had hurt me, but fuck, they had allowed me to hurt *her* in every way possible. I would never forgive them for that.

But I didn't know what to do next.

Did I want to be with her? That was the big question. I wasn't sure, and I didn't know if I would ever get that opportunity. I didn't deserve Myra. I never had. And when I turned my back on her so easily, I had proven that I didn't deserve her. It didn't matter that I felt I had a reason given the evidence I had seen. I should have talked to her about it. Instead, I pushed her away. Now, I needed to deal with the consequences.

A penance we had been paying in our own ways for years.

I pulled into my garage, got Daisy out, and took the food into the house. I let my puppy do her business in the yard and then fed her before heating my leftovers.

I pulled out a beer and sighed, wondering what my life would have been like had Myra still been in it. I honestly didn't want to think too hard about that, though. Because if I did, I knew it would only depress me more.

My doorbell rang, and I frowned, noticing the time. It wasn't too late, but I figured my family would've messaged before they headed over.

I looked at my phone, saw that no one had texted or called, and went to the door. Myra stood on the other side of it. I swallowed hard and looked at the woman I had once loved, a person I didn't know anymore.

"Hey," she said, looking down at her hands. "I told the girls. We need to talk."

I moved out of the way and let my ex-wife into my house, shutting the door behind us.

We *did* need to talk.

Only I was afraid of what we'd say.

Chapter 10

Myra

I had been in Nate's home before, but now I had a chance to look at everything closer, even if I was distracted. The place was so…Nathan. Or at least the guy I had grown to know over the past year, layered on top of the boy I'd once known. Every room had a large, comfortable chair. There were places to sit and mingle, and areas to read. Nathan had always loved reading. There was a large TV, the same kind that most men seemed to have, but a lot of the furniture was turned towards it in the family area, and there appeared to be another room to sit and talk and perhaps read a book. It looked wonderful, as if it were inviting me to sit down and enjoy.

But I didn't think I could.

"Myra." Nate brought me out of my thoughts. I looked up at him then, peered into his kind eyes, even filled with worry, and felt as if no time had passed. Yet decades stretched between us.

"I was just admiring your home," I said after a moment.

"Oh." He frowned. "You've been here before, at least with the others. But I never really showed you around. You want to see?" he asked.

If it would delay the inevitable questions and the possible fight, perhaps I should say yes.

I nodded, and he looked surprised for a moment before holding out his hand. I looked at it, and he swallowed hard before letting his arm drop.

"I'd love to see your home. I mean, I walked through here, but I was really only in the backyard for the barbecue."

"That's right. And you probably went right by here and through the kitchen to the deck. I have a whole other set of rooms. Speaking of, I need to go check on somebody. It's been a little too quiet."

I frowned and then followed him as he jogged towards an office area, where Daisy was currently chewing on a blanket.

"Daisy, what did I say about blankets?"

He went down on his haunches and held out his hand. "Drop it." Daisy froze and blinked up at me, not paying attention to Nate.

"No, me. Drop it, Daisy." She dropped the blanket and then padded over to him, looking as proud as punch as she licked his face.

"Good girl." He laughed. He picked her up as if she weighed nothing and cuddled her close. Something inside me twinged a little bit. He was way too damn sexy with that puppy in his arms. And I needed to stop having those kinds of thoughts.

"Daisy, meet Myra. Myra, this is Daisy."

"Hello." I held out my hand. The puppy sniffed it, licked it, and then gave me a little doggy smile. "Oh, she's too cute."

"And she knows it. I'm going to put her in her octagon for a bit because she's been a little rambunctious, and I don't want her running through the house breaking things while I show you around and we talk."

"Are you sure you have to?" I asked, hating that he had to put her in time-out because I was here.

"We are in training, and she's still learning her boundaries. Both of us are. Macon left a list."

I laughed at the thought of his vet brother laying out directives. "He would know best."

"So he tells me. Often," he said dryly. He set the

puppy behind a white gate in the shape of an octagon, and I looked around at all her toys neatly put away except for a few for her to chew on. She had a bed, water, and a blanket inside the crate.

"It looks like she has everything she needs."

"And probably more. She's my first, so I've been really bad about spoiling her. Plus, she has enough aunts and uncles who give her things. It gets a little insane. But she'll have enough toys to chew through for the next year—or four." He let out a breath, sounding as nervous as I felt. There was comfort in that, even though I knew the inevitable was coming. "Anyway, upstairs is the guest bath, a couple of bedrooms. My master bedroom is on the other side of the house."

"It's a beautiful home, Nathan."

He jolted, and I cursed myself. I had been so good about not calling him by his full first name recently, and yet I had done it to my friends, and now to his face. He didn't like it when I did, because it reminded him of before. And I didn't like it that the word sounded so familiar and was so comfortable on my tongue. I didn't need that reminder.

I met his gaze, trying to find some sense of normalcy in a situation that was anything but ordinary. "I truly love your home. It's very you. It has all kinds of places to read, and lots of photos of your family."

Nathan put his hands into his pockets and rocked

back on his heels. "I work from home, so I do my best to make sure I have places that are for work and those for reading. Sometimes they blend, but I do my best to keep them separate. The photos and things are all Arden's doing."

"Oh?"

"After the accident, we realized that my home wasn't very homey. It was pretty much a place for me to sleep after long hours at work. So, when I bought this place after the settlement, Arden made sure it was a home, rather than just a place to rest my head."

"I'm so sorry you were hurt."

He swallowed hard. "And I'm sorry I hurt you."

I let out a shuddering breath and looked down at my hands. "I don't know what to do with this. What are we supposed to do?"

"Come into the living room. Let's talk."

"You're right. We do need to talk."

I followed him to the living room, wondering how I was supposed to speak when he was so close. That had always been my problem. He filled my brain with this white noise that reminded me of the past. When we were younger, that same thrum had filled me, though it had nothing to do with anger and everything to do with him. I had fallen hard, and far too fast. And there had been no going back. And now, we were in completely different stages of our lives. What were we supposed to do?

As we entered the room, I noticed the beer and ribs and side dishes on the coffee table.

"You were eating."

He looked down at the plate and shrugged. "I was going to try. I went over to Arden's after I invited the family there—"

That made me snort. "You invited everyone to Arden's?"

"I like her house. I wasn't sure I'd be able to tell them everything if I was sitting in my own home, stressing out."

"I went over to Hazel's place."

"So, we needed to get away from home to share the news."

I nodded and took a deep breath. "I told the others."

He paused, studying my face. I didn't know what he saw there, as I didn't know what I felt. "Are you okay?"

"I don't think that's the right question to ask," I answered honestly.

"What did the girls say?" he asked.

"They weren't upset. I thought they might disown me or something."

"I thought that was going to be my line regarding my siblings," he said, relief in his tone.

"They don't hate us?" I asked, afraid of what the answer would be.

Confusion spread over his face, and he shook his head. "They could never hate you, Myra. I don't think they quite understand why we kept it a secret, though."

"I'm not sure I do either, at least not back then."

He nodded. "We were young and stupid."

"Being young and stupid can't be an excuse for everything. But I can use it for now."

He swallowed hard, and I watched his throat work. I did my best not to think about it. It was so hard to do when he was right there. Everything was different now. And I hated that I knew I could fall again if I weren't careful. Because this was Nate. It had always been Nate.

"My family just told me I needed to clean up my mess. And not fuck up again. They're on your side in this." He paused. "Not that there are sides. Because there shouldn't be." He moved forward. I froze, but I didn't step back. When he reached out and cupped my cheek, I wondered if I should move away. If I should run.

"I'm so sorry."

"You already said that," I said icily. Ice was my only defense against him. It always had been.

"Arden told me I needed to make sure you understood that I was sorry. But that I should show you and not simply tell you. I'm trying to figure out exactly what that means and how to do it."

"I don't know what it means either." A pause. "Nate. You believed my parents. You mentioned photos before, but I didn't know what you meant. But you believed them. In my mind, you believed them too easily."

"I shouldn't have."

"I don't know. If I had seen photos of you with another woman, I might've believed the lies, too." I let out a breath. "You have to understand, though. My parents did their best to always tell me what I should do. They put me on my college track, and when I tried to defy them and go to a different school, they ensured that I declared for the major they insisted upon."

"I remember. But you're an artist now, Myra."

"Yet I nearly earned the economics degree they wanted. Instead, I went for business so I could run my own life and career. I took art classes on the side and continued doing what I loved. My grandmother pushed me to do what I wanted." My voice broke at the mention of her, and he brushed his thumb across my cheek.

"I'm so sorry you lost her, Myra."

"I don't want to talk about her right now. I can't, Nate."

"I understand."

"Nate," I whispered and then took a step back. "I can't think when you're touching me."

"That's always been our problem," he muttered.

"Yes, it's always been a problem of ours. But not our only one. My parents twisted everything. They did their best to ensure that I was reliant on them and was the perfect daughter. And when I didn't turn out to be, they broke everything around me so I had to crawl back to them. They provided the only path to my sanity. And I didn't find my way out until almost too late. But by then, they'd already shattered everything I had with you. We were *married*, Nathan."

"I remember."

"And it was the most idiotic and romantic and amazing thing I've ever done in my life. We were still figuring out what it meant to be married. We were so young. We didn't even have a chance to find our path together because my parents stepped in and did their normal manipulating. And we both fell for it. If you would've just let me know why—"

He leaned forward. "I thought that I wasn't good enough for you. That we married too young, that it was a mistake. And that you were going back to what was good for you."

It felt like a cold slap after so many years. "And you didn't let me decide what was good for me."

"I know. I'm so fucking sorry. I wish I could go back and change all of that."

"The thing is, Nathan, would things have been different?" I asked.

His gaze shot up to mine. "What do you mean?"

"If we had stayed together, if we had moved past the lies my family told, would we have remained married? We were so young and still finding ourselves even while falling for each other. Would I have found what makes me whole? Would you have become the man you are today?"

The silence between us was palpable, and I could see Nate's mind working as mine struggled to catch up.

"We can never go back," he said.

"We can't."

"But I can do everything in my power to make sure you understand that I'm sorry as we try to find a way to move forward."

"And what do you want to move forward to?" I asked, my breath growing shallow as he moved forward again.

"I don't know, Myra. But I need to do something. Will you let me?"

"Let you do what?" I asked.

And then his lips were on mine, and I didn't push him away.

I should have. This was not talking. This was not what we should be doing to find our truth and the answers we needed.

And yet my arms moved around him, and it was as if no time had passed.

This was the man I had loved. The boy I had fallen for and then married and promised my life to. And his mouth was on mine now. I sank into him, needing more.

I kissed him back, but when his hands skimmed down my back to cup my butt, pulling me against him, I nearly swooned. I could feel the long, thick line of his erection, and memories flooded back. How he made me feel, the way he felt inside me. I knew we should stop.

This was a mistake. Yet, I didn't push him away.

"I don't want to talk," I whispered.

"We don't have to," he said before biting my lip and then kissing down my neck.

"Just this once," I whispered.

"This is crazy," he breathed.

"Shut up and kiss me."

His lips claimed mine. This couldn't be happening. This wasn't real. It had to be a dream. Or maybe it was one last time, and then we could walk away. I didn't know. I couldn't think. I'd missed Nate so damn much.

It really was as if no time had passed. This was the man I had married, the person I'd wanted to be with for the rest of my life. So, when he kissed me harder and tugged on my hair, I pulled on his shirt. He shifted so he could help me strip his torso, and then my hands were on his bare flesh, the heat of him searing my palms.

"When did you get so big?" I asked against his lips and felt him smile.

"I have a joke for that," he whispered, then issued a deep chuckle that rumbled through me.

"You have so much muscle now. You weren't scrawny before, but…wow."

"I was a boy before, Myra. Now, I'm a man. Is that fact going to be too much for you?"

"I don't want to think. Don't ask me questions."

"Is this going to be another mistake?" he asked.

"If it is, it's one I want to make." I knew those words were probably a lie. This was idiotic. It wasn't what I'd come here for. It would probably only make things worse. But I kissed him, and when he lifted me off my feet, I wrapped my legs around his waist, needing more.

"Just once," I whispered.

"Once."

He shoved my back against the wall, my skirt riding up to my hips. I arched into him, needing him, kissing him, forgetting the rest of the world.

This was the man I had loved, and it was everything. If we could pretend, then we could walk away… This could be goodbye. I kept rationalizing all of this to myself, but it made no sense. It didn't need to. I pulled at his pants, and he undid his belt buckle and pushed his jeans down to his knees. He slid his hands between my thighs, and I moaned, his fingers spearing me.

"Already wet for me, baby."

"Shut up."

"Oh, so you're feisty now?"

"I was always this way." I bit his lip, and he'd growled, capturing my lips again as he moved those two fingers. I arched, my body shaking as his thumb pressed against my clit, his fingers curling to rub the tangle of nerves inside me.

He pumped in and out, his hands working hard enough to make me shake. I reached between us, trying to touch him, but it was too much. I came on his hand, his name a rasp on my lips as my legs shook. And then his fingers slid out, and I could finally grasp him. He was hard and thick, bigger than I remembered.

"You didn't grow here, did you?"

He laughed. "No, still the same size. Damn, you're so fucking beautiful, Myra. I always loved your curves, but I swear to God, I could lick you up."

"Not now. I can't wait, Nathan." I didn't say the word *later*. Didn't say "*next time*." Because this could be the only time. I needed to languish in this mistake and not think about the future. And so, I gripped him and positioned him at my entrance. He met my gaze before slamming home. I gasped, both of us freezing at the riot of sensations. Nate was warm and so wide that I had to stretch to accommodate him.

And yet, this felt familiar. As if we had done it a thousand times before with no time in between. I could barely catch my breath before he pulled out of me and then pressed back in.

I met him thrust for thrust, my lips on his, my skirt moving farther up my body as he cupped my ass and spread me. He pounded me against the wall, and I scraped my fingernails down his back, leaving gouges. I couldn't help it. I needed him.

When I came again, I bit his shoulder, and he threw back his head and shouted my name, filling me as he came, as well.

In the aftermath, the coolness of the air-conditioned room chilled my body, and my sweat-slick skin grew clammy. I couldn't look at him. I couldn't do anything. Instead, I froze against the wall, my body still holding onto him, his cock still hard inside me, and I tried to take a deep breath.

"Myra," he whispered.

"I need to clean up," I said, my voice wavering.

"Shit. Myra."

"If you say you're sorry, I'll slap you. Please, pull out of me. I need to clean up."

So he did, oh so carefully. My panties were shoved to the side—we hadn't even stripped each other entirely. I was still wearing my bra, for God's sake.

This was the heat and the temptation that had gotten us into trouble before. And here we were, making another mistake. All because I hadn't wanted to speak, hadn't wanted to think. And I'd thought this action might be worth the consequences.

I was not the cool and calculated Myra that I showed to the world. I was now the temptress and the sin that had gotten me into trouble before. I didn't want to hate myself, but I couldn't help but despise the gravity of my mistakes.

Nate was back in an instant as I fixed my skirt, and he helped me clean up. Still, I stood there, looking at him with his pants undone, his body sweaty. I knew there was evidence of what we had done on his back, my fingernails having left marks. But I couldn't even look at him.

"I'm clean. You're the only person I've ever not used a condom with."

I hadn't even thought about it. What the hell was wrong with me? I'd never had sex with someone without a condom before—other than Nathan. And at that point, we were married.

I cleared my throat. "I'm clean, as well. I can show you the reports."

"Same."

"I need to go."

"Myra."

I shook my head, not meeting his gaze. "No. I need to go. I just…this can't happen again."

"Myra—"

"Goodbye, Nathan."

I picked up my bag, and I ran.

And once again, he let me.

Chapter 11

Nate

I'd given her twelve hours, and I thought that was enough time. I knew from Macon that Myra wasn't taking care of Joshua this morning, so I figured she should be home. If not, I would track her down, and we would talk. Because if we didn't, I was afraid my head might fall right off my shoulders.

How the hell had we gone from trying to understand what had happened in our past to having sex in my fucking living room? It made no goddamn sense. Yes, I was attracted to her, but that didn't mean I'd needed to bang her right there.

It was a mistake, a lack of judgment on both our parts. And we had to talk about it.

But, Jesus Christ, despite that, I wanted to do it again. And that was the problem—one of many. Being with Myra again was like a thousand moments in time wrapped up in a necessary breath. I hadn't thought to be with her again. I had never allowed myself to believe that it would ever happen. It couldn't. I'd hated her at one point. But I had been wrong. I hadn't known the truth. And I knew that I couldn't hate her. Ever.

I could only hate myself. But now we had slept together, and I didn't know what to do about it. We needed to talk. Again. But I knew how well that had gone before.

I had told my family members to talk to their significant others when things got insane, that communication always had to be the most important thing. So, I would live up to what I told others, even if it felt like I was raking myself over hot coals. And I had yet to figure out exactly how to grovel the way I should.

I stood on Myra's porch, not knowing if she was home for sure because her car could be in the garage. I knocked on the door and let out a breath, not knowing what to say, and hoping to hell that she was home, while also praying she wasn't. This could be Schrodinger's house. If no one ever came to the door, perhaps she was hiding from me, or not here at all.

Myra opened the door as I was having my existential crisis. She stared at me, her eyes a bit puffy, her lips swollen as if she had bitten them rather than having my mouth on hers like I wanted.

"I should have known you would be here this morning."

I swallowed hard. "May I come in?"

"I suppose you should." She took a step back, and I walked in, doing my best not to touch her or brush against her. Because if I did, I was afraid what I might do. It was hard to keep from touching her. I wanted to hold her close and pretend like our past hadn't happened. That, somehow, we were moving beyond all the pain that had broken us. Only I knew that was a dream, and one I didn't even want.

And that was the crux of it, wasn't it?

"Do you want some coffee?" she asked, and that's when I realized that she was holding a mug. She had on a long sleeve cotton shirt and jeans with holes in the thighs and knees. There were paint splatters on her wrists, as well as on her hips. Her hair was piled on the top of her head, although some of the layers were a bit short and fell around her face, the blond pieces making it look like a halo.

She was both my fall and my salvation. And I was the one left wanting.

"I would love some coffee," I said after a moment.

She nodded tightly. "Then let's get you some. Honestly, I'm glad you're here. We can be adults about this. We aren't children anymore."

"You're right. And I think coffee would probably be the best thing right now because I sort of chugged mine before I got here. It might've scalded my throat."

She smiled half-heartedly, but it didn't reach her eyes. We were off to a rocking start so far.

I followed her into her kitchen and studied the lines of her home. It was beautiful, light in every corner, and places for photos and art and so many of the things that spoke of the person Myra was now, but I also caught glimpses of the Myra I had known before.

There were no photos of her family other than her grandmother and a few female cousins I knew she liked. I didn't see her parents or that annoying cousin, Roland. I didn't see memories of her college year with me. But there *were* photos of the pact sisters. And of Joshua and the kittens.

So many memories of when she was happy, when she was the Myra she was becoming, the one I desperately craved and wanted to get to know, even if I knew it wasn't my place or my right to do so.

Her kitchen was white with light granite and cabinets that looked almost modern country. I had seen a few HGTV shows, but Arden had decorated my place. I didn't know what to call Myra's home or style, other than comfortable. Not exactly warm, the coolness of the metal and the reclaimed wood and sharp lines of some of the pieces wouldn't scream *home* to some. But I saw it, and I knew that it was pure Myra. Her home. So, while others might not see warmth, I did. Because beneath the icy exterior, there was a warmth to the woman. The person I had loved.

And, deep down, I was afraid I still loved her.

"Here you go." She handed me a gray mug with hearts etched into the side.

"This looks homemade." I looked down at the mug in my hand.

"Joshua made it, actually," Myra said with a smile.

I looked down at the piece of pottery that looked nothing like something a child would make.

"Seriously? When I was his age, anything I made had enough holes in it to not be usable."

Myra snorted. "I did most of it, but he helped. Had his little hands in mine when I was at the potter's wheel."

"So, you throw pottery?" I asked, not knowing that little tidbit regarding the woman I'd thought I knew so well all those years ago.

"Sometimes. I work with mixed metals and other

materials, too. However, oil on canvas is still my bread and butter. Cliché for the people of my hometown."

"I would think that would be watercolors."

She smiled at that. "True, after luncheons and then brandies after dinner. Okay, so that's a historical romance and not so much the elite of California."

"I've seen your pieces," I blurted.

Her eyes widened. "Really?"

"Other than a couple of the ones I saw around your home just now? Yes. Hazel has one."

"She does." Myra smiled. "I'm working on ones for Paris and Dakota. Joshua has a small painting in his room. I also have something in mind for Arden, but it takes me a bit to get there. I have commissions and a show coming up. With everything happening so quickly with the attack and our friends being in danger, it's been hard to get in the mood to create hope and happiness. My art's gone a little darker than I want lately, and while that's fine for an art show, it's not the best thing to put into something for your friend's wall."

I took a sip of the coffee and nearly choked.

"What's wrong?" she asked.

"Nothing," I said.

Her eyes widened, and then she let out a breath. "I didn't even think about it. I know exactly how you like your coffee, and I made it without even thinking. Do you have the same tastes?"

"Yes. One sugar, one cream. Like we had at that diner."

"I loved that place. They had the best chicken fried steak with biscuits and so much gravy. Something I cannot have any more, unless I want to clog my arteries and work out for an extra hour the next day. But it was so good."

"I was sad when the place closed." I took another sip of the coffee, trying to wash down the memories.

"I hadn't heard," Myra said, sadness filling her eyes.

"A couple of years after you left. The owner passed away, and his kids didn't want to run the place anymore. There's another diner there now, and I hear it does just as well. I never went, though."

"After I left…" she said, her voice trailing off. "I should have stayed to talk to you. I should have told you what happened, or asked you what happened rather. But I let my parents bully me like usual, and I left. I signed the divorce papers, and I was so hurt, I didn't even talk to you."

I set down my coffee and shook my head, then moved forward so I was close enough to read her face. It was so hard to get a bead on her emotions these days, but I was learning. Though I wasn't sure how much I should. What were we doing? Did I want this to progress? Or did I want for us to remain only friends?

I wasn't sure what the answer was, but regardless, I needed to beg for forgiveness and work on that groveling.

"You left because I was an idiot. Because I believed your parents without doubting what I saw the way I should have."

"I wish I could have seen those photos," she ground out.

I swallowed the bile rising up my throat and then shook my head. "You don't. You really don't."

"I want to say I can't believe they did that, but I can. Those are the same people who didn't even tell me that my grandmother died. They are cruel, and so easy about it. It's as if the lies and the audacity just drip right off their tongues, as if they don't have to worry about the consequences of their actions. And maybe that's true. Both of my parents come from money and have never had to worry about anything but what vacation they want to take next. They got their degrees to work in their jobs—my mother with charities, my father with the family business. I was never once told that I should follow in his footsteps. That was Roland, my cousin, the one you met."

I ground my teeth. "Yeah, I remember him."

"He's the one following in my father's footsteps.

Because he was born a boy."

"But did you ever want to do what your father does?" I asked, wondering why we'd never talked about this before.

"No, I didn't." She laughed.

"You don't regret the fact that your father never groomed you for that?"

"They told me what degree to get so I could better help with the charities my mother ran. So I could take her place. It's a hard business, one that doesn't pay, but it's good work, even if it's mostly about trying to elevate your social standing."

"That's a whole world that I have nothing to do with," I said.

"And I loved that you didn't." She bit her lip.

"I always felt like I wasn't good enough for you because I wasn't from those circles."

"That was never the case, Nathan."

"But it's what I felt. And I didn't talk to you about it because I didn't want to make things weird or hard for you. And that's on me."

"I want you to know that I didn't fall for you because you weren't part of that set. You know? The girl who falls for the bad boy so she doesn't have to worry about her past?"

That made me snort.

"We are not that couple. We never were. We fell for

the people we thought each other was, not the people we thought we were running from."

"I'd almost forgotten how many times you used to see to the crux of the matter. You were always so brilliant."

"Were?" I asked, raising a brow.

Myra rolled her eyes. "I'm sure you still think you're brilliant."

I put my hand over my heart. "Ouch." I let out a breath. "I don't know how you're ever going to forgive me, or if I even want your forgiveness. Because I don't deserve it."

"You don't need to beat yourself up over it anymore," Myra said, setting her coffee cup on the counter before pacing the kitchen. "That's what my parents want. They want us to hate each other. They want me to be put in my place. Even if they've pushed me completely out of the family as much as they can, they still want me for certain things. And you being out of my life is probably part of that. Even if it's deep down."

I frowned. "I'm going to ask something, and I don't want you to get angry."

She froze, her brow rising. "I can't promise that. Especially when you add a disclaimer."

"Fine. Did you sleep with me to make your parents angry?" I asked and then groaned.

"Nathan Brady. Seriously?"

"See? It was the stupidest thought. I don't even know why I said it."

"No, I didn't. And I don't know why I slept with you, which sounds stupid. We had sex. As we were fighting, and sort of figuring out what the hell we were doing, we had sex in your living room or reading room or whatever the hell you want to call it. Against the wall. Without a condom. That was so stupid, Nate. Not only because of the lack of protection, but because of everything else."

"I know." I ran my hands over my hair. "I have done many stupid things in my life, Myra. Most of them having to do with you."

"Ouch," she said, the look in her eyes teasing.

"You know what I mean."

"Oddly enough, I do," she said, picking up her coffee again.

"I took so long to figure out who I was. Somewhere along the way, I lost you. And I will forever be sorry for that. But, here we are. We are so connected, and we can't change that. Now, we have to figure out how to coexist in this world we created."

"We shouldn't have sex again."

Nate winced. "If you're going to put it out there like that."

"Nathan," she said with a laugh.

I sobered. "I missed you calling me that."

"You're not the boy I used to call Nathan."

"And you're not the girl I married." I paused. "And that's good. We grew apart, yes. But we're different people now. And given that we know the truth, and everybody knows about our past, I think we should find a way to live with that."

"That's what I was thinking," she agreed. "We need to start over. Have a clean slate where we don't antagonize one another when we're in the same room. We'll figure out exactly who we are to each other within the boundaries we've already set in terms of our friendship. We can't take back what was done, but maybe we can move forward, maturely and responsibly."

I studied her face and knew she had rehearsed those words.

And thank God for it because I had no idea what to say. "Mature and responsible."

"Since we are older, we should try that."

I swallowed hard. "I can do that. I don't want to be the angry person I was becoming around you. And I don't want to lament our mistakes. Plus, I don't want you to leave my life. Even when we hated each other, I liked having you there. Even as it was bad for me."

"That's the most twisted thing you've ever said," she said on a laugh. "But the weird thing is, I agree."

"I'm going to spend the time that we have, making up for what happened," I added.

She shook her head. "You don't have to, Nathan."

I moved forward and touched her face. Her lips parted, and all I wanted to do was lean down and kiss her. But I didn't.

"I have to. Even if it's selfish of me, I need to make it up to you."

"I don't know if that makes sense."

I shook my head. "Nothing about this makes sense. But we're going to move forward and start fresh. And that means I need to be able to look at myself in the mirror and not remember every horrible thing I did."

"We'll figure out who we are and what we are together. And we won't hate each other anymore."

I didn't move closer to press my lips to hers, to taste her, so I pulled away and put my hands into my pockets.

"We'll start over."

She held out her hand, and I laughed before sliding my hand into hers.

A handshake to start a friendship.

And yet I knew that wasn't truly the case. Because we had done far more than hold hands or shake. Eventually, we would have to talk about that. But first, I would hold her hand. The rest would have to come along the way.

Chapter 12

Myra

"WE ARE HERE TODAY TO DISCUSS A MATTER OF GREAT importance."

Dakota snickered at my side, and I glared at her before doing the same to Paris.

"Are you giving a sermon now?" I asked, adopting my most haughty tone.

"Only for you, darling." Paris winked.

"If you're done making fun of her," Dakota began, "we have a few things to go over."

"Mainly, let's talk about you and Nate." Hazel gave me a pointed look, and I sighed, knowing they had all come over to my place for a reason. Not because of the pact, or because of a promise, but because of what was inherent in who we were.

"There's so much to talk about. I don't even know where to begin, so I'd rather not say anything at all," I said after a moment, my words tumbling out one after the other.

"Why don't you start from the beginning?" Hazel reached out to grab my hand. "We love you. And I'm not going to speak for everyone, but I will say that I forgive you for what you withheld. We've all had our secrets, and I understand."

"Same here," Dakota said.

"I mean, I will be bitter, but that's only because I need something in your con column for when I'm trying to get out of things when I screw up," Paris said, her face carefully neutral before she cracked up.

I shook my head, relief spreading through me much faster than I thought possible. I hadn't expected them to forgive me. Sure, they might've said something along those lines, but they were also shocked about what had happened. Now, they'd had a couple of days to contemplate what I had told them fully, and I felt like these were their honest reactions.

I wanted to curl up into a ball and cry.

And because of that, I didn't allow myself to do it. I only cried when I couldn't hold back. And I had spent years not being a person who shed tears at the drop of a hat. I kept doing it lately, and I wasn't happy about it.

"You asked us over here, and I assume it's not so you can apologize again," Paris said.

"I could if you need me to," I said honestly.

"You don't."

I looked at Hazel, the woman I had known the longest, who I was the closest to, and I wanted to wrap my arms around her and never let go.

"Okay, since I last spoke to you, there have been...developments."

All of them leaned forward, and I swallowed hard, wishing I had wine in my hand. But I also knew I needed to do this sober, and not rely on anything but my determination.

"What kind of developments?" Dakota asked.

"The juicy kind?" Paris asked, and I cringed.

"Wow, that brought up visuals I don't even want to imagine," Hazel said, and we all laughed, the tension sliding away ever so slightly.

"Just say it in one quick burst." Dakota met my gaze, and I let out a breath.

"Nate and I slept together."

"You're serious?" Hazel asked.

"Wow," Dakota mouthed.

"You mean since the divorce?" Paris asked, straight to the point as always.

"As in right after I told you guys." I clarified.

Hazel blinked.

"We had sex. Against a wall. And we were still wearing our clothes." I let out a groan and put my hands over my face, hunching over my knees.

The girls were silent for a moment before they all started speaking at once. I only caught a few words, something about wow and oh my God, and a question: how was it?

I snorted and shook my head. "I don't want to get into the particulars."

"You're welcome to get into the particulars." Paris winked. "So, let me get this straight, you guys fight constantly, you finally tell us that you guys were married and got divorced in short order, and then you slept together?"

I nodded, swallowing hard. "That about sums it up."

"What does it mean?" Dakota asked.

"It means nothing, other than the fact that I wanted to be clear with all of you that it has to mean nothing. Nate and I shook on it. We're friends."

Paris snorted.

"Oh, so that's what they're calling it these days?" Hazel asked, her voice sly.

"Stop it." I could feel my cheeks heating up as I blushed, and I shook my head. "It was an accident."

"So, he just fell into you over and over again?" Paris asked, her voice dry.

"Now there's an image," Dakota said.

"Anyway," I cut in as they all started laughing with one another, "it was fun, it cut the tension, and we're never doing it again. We had a handshake after we talked about it the next morning and we both said we wouldn't do it again. We're friends, and we'll make this work."

"You're going to make being friends work…"

I nodded at Hazel. "We have to. We've already gone through so much because of how young we were and my parents being who they are. It's too much to get over. But we can try to be friends. Because we're all so connected, and I don't want to interfere with that."

"And what about your heart?" Dakota asked softly.

"What of it? There was no heart involved in what Nate and I did."

I knew those words were a lie, but I wasn't going to let myself call them anything but the truth.

The girls nodded at me and swallowed hard.

"Okay," Hazel added, her voice low. "I'm glad you told us. Now, there are no more awkward secrets, though I am going to have to try and imagine exactly how you had sex with all of your clothes on against a wall."

Paris grinned like a cat with a canary. "Oh, there are ways."

I cringed. "Please, stop. I have to face Prior at our next meal, and I don't need to picture that."

"Oh, and we have to picture Nate?" Dakota asked.

I groaned into my hands again. "See? This is why Nate and I shouldn't do that again. We need to find a way to be friends. Having sex changes everything."

"It does," Hazel added. "And I totally understand. If you guys can find some peace, then I'm all for it. I just don't want you to get hurt."

I swallowed the lump in my throat and reached out and gripped her hand. The others were near me, and I leaned into them, my circle, my pact sisters.

"I love you guys. And I'm glad that everything's out in the open. But I'm never going to be with Nate. Not again. That ship sailed, sank, and was lost at sea. There's no extra rowboat out there for me."

"You have completely killed that metaphor," Paris joked.

"Perhaps. But I wanted to make sure you understood. I'm never going to be with Nate. And I think I'm finally okay with that."

The girls gave each other a look, but thankfully

they didn't say anything. Instead, I leaned into my sisters and told myself that I hadn't just lied.

Nate

"YOU DID WHAT?" Arden asked, and I took another sip of my beer, swallowing hard.

"I had sex with Myra."

"Recently?" my sister asked again, her voice going high-pitched.

"Hey, I think you're going to hurt Jasper's ears if you keep screeching like that."

"Jasper's fine," she said while running her hand over her dog's head.

"Fine, then Daisy's ears."

My puppy sat at my feet and looked at me adoringly.

"Stop changing the subject. You slept with Myra?"

I sighed, set down my beer, and then picked up Daisy so she could lick at my chin. "Yes. Just the once. It's never going to happen again. We shook on it."

Arden blinked at me. "Is that a phrase I don't know

about? Is shaking a new thing that the kids do these days?"

"We're twins, dork. Why would I know what the kids do these days and not you? And stop being weird."

"You're the one being weird. You had sex with your ex-wife, and you're just casually bringing it up in conversation? Do the brothers know?"

I shook my head and scratched under Daisy's chin. "No. I'll let them know later. Only because Myra is telling her girls, and we don't want any more secrets. But in the end, it doesn't matter. We're moving on as friends now that we have a new idea of what the truth is, and we don't have to worry about hurting each other again."

"That's a load of crap," Arden said.

"What?" I asked, confused as I set Daisy down so she could play with Jasper.

"You can't say that you're just going to be friends after you slept together. You guys have a tangled history. Even if you hadn't made a truce to walk away, someone's going to get hurt. They always do."

I shook my head. "No, we're going to be careful."

"So careful that you slept with her?" Arden asked, and I sighed.

"It's fine, Arden."

"Now you're lying to yourself *and* me."

"So what if I am?" I asked, exhausted. "I need

everything to be fine. I know it's cliché to say we didn't mean for it to turn out as it did, but it's true. We just fell into each other. I didn't mean to sleep with her; it just happened. And it's never going to happen again."

Arden stared at me for a long moment, and I sighed. It looked as if she was going to yell at me before she closed her eyes and let out a slow breath.

"I love you. You're my twin and a part of my soul. But I don't want you to get hurt. This situation is complicated. Everything about it is."

I reached for my beer and took another swig so I could get my thoughts in order. "I know. I know it's complicated, and I know that neither of us actually has a handle on what we fucking want in our lives. But we do know that if we don't get it together, we'll end up hurting each other. We'll hurt our friends and family. And I don't want that. I don't want somebody to get hurt because I'm an idiot."

My sister looked at me, dark circles under her eyes, her body so frail. She'd had another flare recently, and it was taking its toll on her. But she was here. Making decisions and being a positive force in the world.

And if she could do that, then so could I.

"I love you, baby brother."

"And I love you, baby sister."

"I like Myra, Nate. I did before, as well. I honestly

never thought she could do what her parents accused her of. It was so out of character for her."

I winced and took another sip of my beer. "It was. That's why it broke me."

"And I know you well enough to realize it must have taken something genuine for you to believe that she could have done something like that."

"I should've kept the pictures to show her, and we could have gotten over it. But I think the damage was already done by then."

"You didn't want to keep pictures of the woman you loved having sex with someone else," she said bitterly.

"True, but I still handled everything poorly."

"So, have you groveled enough yet?" she asked.

I shook my head. "Not nearly enough."

"And that's the right answer. You're never going to be with her again?" she asked, her gaze on mine.

"I don't think I can. I think we're past that. We missed our window. We made so many mistakes. We don't get a second or a fourth chance."

"But the first time you guys finally had some barriers knocked down, you went for each other. You had hope, even in those most precious of moments. Are you sure you can walk away from that?"

I set my beer down again and looked at the dogs curled up in a ball, already napping on the kitchen floor. "I don't know if I have a choice, Arden. I don't know what I feel anymore. It's all tangled up in a mess that's ugly and complicated."

"Sometimes, love is ugly and complicated. It's what you get out of it that makes it's true purpose."

"But it's not just me. I hurt her so much, Arden. I don't think I deserve her."

"The first thing you need to do is find out if you want to be a man who deserves her. And then you have to find a way to be him."

"And that's the crux of it, isn't it?" I asked, letting out a breath.

"Figure it out. I know you can do it. I love you, Nate. I don't want to see you hurt again."

"And I don't want to be the one that causes pain."

And that was my problem. And something I still didn't have a solution for.

Chapter 13

Myra

It had been a week since my reality had shifted once more, and I still didn't have my feet on the ground. A week since my parents were on my doorstep, along with my cousin, lies on their tongues, and the truth buried under miles of deceit. I felt like I was still trying to come up for air, the world suffocating me. But I *could* find my way. I had to. That didn't make what I had to do today any easier, though.

The girls had offered to come with me. Even Dakota had said she would hand the reins to her cafe over to one of her staff members so she could be by my side. But I had told them I could do this on my own—that I needed to.

I wasn't sure that any of them believed me. I wasn't sure I believed myself.

However, I did not have a choice. I needed to walk through the doors in front of me and face my reality.

My grandmother was dead. And I hadn't had a chance to say goodbye, nor had I been able to grieve. And now I had to deal with the death, the paperwork of that, and the stench of bureaucracy so I could face the future. I wasn't comfortable with what I had to do, but I had told my family I would be here, and that meant I was. I would fulfill my promises, unlike anything they had ever done for me.

I knew I needed to stop thinking so negatively; it wasn't good for my health. But that didn't make this any easier. I took a deep breath and stepped to the doors, the automatic glass sliding out of my way as I did.

A young, blond woman with her hair neatly shorn sat at the front desk, a pleasant smile on her face.

"Hello, how may I help you?"

"My name is Myra West. I'm here to see Mr. Ongard."

"Ah, yes. He's waiting for you and the rest of your party in his office."

I frowned and looked down at my watch. "I wasn't aware that I was late. Sorry."

"No, you're early, the others were just a little earlier than you." I saw the strain in her eyes at the mention of *the others*—namely my parents and whatever cousins were around—and I hoped that they hadn't made this morning too hard on her already. I knew it was difficult enough as it was.

"If you'll show me where to go…?" I asked her.

"Oh, of course. Right this way."

I followed the woman down the hall, trying to keep my breath steady. As soon as I took my first step, I knew this was real. My grandmother would no longer call me. I wouldn't see her again. She wouldn't finally move out to Colorado to stay with me for the rest of her retirement. When my grandfather died, I had lost a part of myself. But I knew Grandma had lost more of herself. Regardless, she had survived a decade without him.

And now, I needed to survive without her.

"Here you are, I'm so sorry for your loss."

I nodded at her and made my way through the door, my head held high. I would be the icy queen today. Not only to protect my heart from what was to come but also as armor against the people I did not want to see.

"It's about time you got here," Roland said, looking down at his phone.

"I wasn't aware we were meeting so early."

"You never did apologize for anything, did you?" my mother asked, sighing as she looked down at her watch.

"There's no need for me to apologize. But I'm glad we're all here so we can get through these next steps quickly."

"You want to get this over with quickly?" my father asked. "Do you already know what's about to be said?"

I shook my head, taking the only empty seat in the room. It was a smaller, ornate chair that was set apart from the others, and I couldn't help but feel a little disconnected. There was a small sofa in the corner, as well, but no one had taken that.

I heard quick footsteps behind me, and I looked at the door. My eyes widened as Lacey walked through. Lacey was another of my cousins. She lived in Wyoming with her husband and three children. I liked her, though I didn't see her often. Her parents, another aunt on my mother's side, had disowned her long before my parents tried to do the same with me.

"I was afraid I was going to be late. Traffic on I-25 was worse than usual."

She came forward as I stood up, and she kissed my cheek. "I'm so sorry. I know she was always the closest to you. I didn't hear until…well, it doesn't matter. I'm sorry."

Tears pricked my eyes, and it felt odd to have what I considered almost an ally in this. I had forgotten Lacey, not because she was cruel or not worth remembering. She wasn't a part of my life. Hadn't been when we were children either. Her parents had moved out to New York when we were kids, and she had only visited occasionally to see our grandparents. When she got pregnant during college and married the love of her life, they moved out to Wyoming to be with his family. They now owned a ranch, and I knew they were doing relatively well. She lived so close to me, yet I hadn't seen her in ages.

I needed to change that.

"Let's talk after this," I whispered, aware that everyone was staring.

"Yes, I'd like that." Her eyes filled ever so slightly before she blinked the tears away, a small smile on her face that was real.

"I see we're all here," a man with graying hair at his temples and a firm jaw said as he walked through another door behind the desk area. "Hello, I'm Mr. Ongard," the man said, holding out his hand to Lacey and me. I shook it, grateful that he seemed to be a no-nonsense type of man, but he had kind eyes. I had learned long ago to read the kindness in someone's eyes.

"Now that we're all settled, let's begin the proceedings."

An intern came in behind the lawyer, holding a stack of papers and a tablet, presumably to take notes.

"I will read the will as stated, and any questions can be asked after. Please keep your remarks until the end so we can get through this. I know this is a tough time for all of you, and it's completely understandable if you need me to talk over things and elaborate on the points afterward. But once we get through the main items, we can get through it all. Again, I'm sorry for your loss."

"Thank you," I said, not meaning to say the words aloud. My mother narrowed her eyes at me since no one else had spoken. But Lacey was angled behind me on the couch, and I could feel her presence, a warmth I hadn't known I needed. I was glad that I hadn't brought anyone with me, even though Nate's face filled my mind at the thought because bringing anybody but myself would have been a shield the others would have seen as a weakness. The idea that I had to think those thoughts when it came to my family hurt, but I didn't dwell on it.

"Okay. Let's begin."

He began reading the will, going over the initial

instructions for the terms of my grandmother's estate. With each word, it was as if he were pounding nails into the coffin—a word for each hammer strike. I would not break down, even though that's all I wanted to do.

"To my daughter, Constance West, I leave my emerald jewelry collection as listed below. May you find warmth in the coolness of the stones."

My mother squeezed my father's hand, and I was glad that she got those pieces. She had always loved them, and though they were beautiful, they weren't my mother's stone. The lawyer named another stone collection for each of my grandmother's daughters before he let out a breath.

"To my niece, Lacey Brennen-Holden, I leave a small trust with the terms listed for her children and grandchildren, with names to be added according to the policy below. Your children will never have to worry about their futures, as I know you once did. You are a shining star, my Lacey. And I love you."

I resisted the urge to turn around as Lacey sobbed, but I would go to her later, and we'd find comfort with one another. We needed to get through this, and I was barely holding on as it was.

"As for the rest of the estate, holdings, monetary accruals, and properties, I leave them to my granddaughter, Myra West." There was a shocked gasp to the side of me and a curse, but I ignored it, my pulse racing.

"As the note reads, 'I trust my Myra to do what is best, to find those who need hope in the darkness and an extra hand. I trust you with all of my heart, and always have.'"

He went on to talk about other items and instructions, but I barely listened. Grandma had left nearly everything to me. I couldn't catch my breath. It didn't make any sense. She had other grandchildren, and she hadn't even mentioned the spouses of *her* children. She had left my mother a small collection of jewelry but nothing else.

"Now, do you have any questions?" the lawyer asked, and Roland growled.

"That's it? When did she change it?"

I looked over at my cousin, the anger in his face so palpable I almost had to lean back in my chair.

"Her will has been stated this way for the past six years."

"That can't be right," my mother said. "She left everything to Myra? Myra left the family."

"I didn't leave. I moved to another state," I corrected, not knowing why I was even arguing.

"What did you do to get into her good graces?" Roland asked.

The lawyer cleared his throat. "We don't need to

be shouting, ladies and gentlemen. We can talk these things over calmly and logically."

"There's no need," my mother spat, standing up on her high heels. My father and Roland followed. "Our lawyers will be contacting you soon to contest this. This is ridiculous. I am her daughter. Not Myra."

"I have the will right here, and it's legally binding. You're welcome to contest it, of course, but your mother was of sound mind when she wrote this and had it finalized."

"What kind of charlatan are you for letting her do this? Myra can't handle that kind of inheritance."

"I'm sitting right here. Grandma Sharon is *gone*. Why can't we simply focus on what we lost? We can work out everything else later." I needed to breathe.

Someone put their hand on my shoulder, and I looked up at Lacey, who gave me a squeeze. I let out a breath. I had to remember that I wasn't alone here. Even if I didn't know Lacey all that well, I trusted her much more than I trusted the others.

"You'll be hearing from my lawyer," my mother repeated before she stormed out, my father and Roland on her tail.

The anger seeped off them, and I stood on shaky legs, looking at the intern and the lawyer, trying to formulate words. "Thank you. I need time to contemplate what just happened."

"Of course. We have your contact information. We'll talk soon. There's a lot of paperwork to go over."

I swallowed hard. "I don't know what I'm supposed to do now," I said.

"Why don't we get you home?" Lacey whispered. "I need to get home to my babies and the ranch, but I'm only a quick drive away if you need me. The lawyer will figure out everything else. I'm sure I'll have a lot of questions, too."

I looked at my cousin and swallowed hard. "Thank you. I just… I don't know what to say."

She reached out and wiped the tears from my face. "We lost Grandma Sharon. I don't think there's anything we should be saying or doing right now."

As the lawyer and intern quietly left us alone, I held onto my cousin, one I didn't know very well and hadn't spoken to in years, and I wept.

By the time we left the office, I was emotionally drained and physically exhausted. I would have countless things to sign and go over before I was even close to finished with all of this.

I had estates to deal with, money I hadn't ever dreamed of having, and countless other small things to work through. I knew right away that I wasn't going to keep every dollar my grandmother left me. I figured that was probably why she had given it to me in the first place. I'd find a way to make things work, even though I knew my family and my parents and cousins would never forgive me for being named as Grandma's heir.

I drove without thinking. When I found myself in front of Nate's house, I let out a small sigh. I couldn't even avoid him when I wanted to. Instead, my subconscious had led me here, and now I would have to see him. I got out of the car as he stood on the porch, Daisy on a leash, currently chewing it as she tugged at him.

"We just finished with a walk, and she had her water, but now she wants to chew. Do you want to come in?" He studied my face, and I swallowed hard before making my way to him. He hugged me tightly, Daisy sliding between us, trying to cuddle and get more love.

"Today sucked," I whispered.

"I'm glad you came."

"I don't know why I'm here."

"We'll figure that out. I'm glad you're here."

He brought me inside, cuddling we close. We got Daisy situated, and she passed out on her little bed in her octagon as soon as she finished drinking water. Nate brought me a glass of ginger ale.

I took a sip and coughed. "Is there whiskey in this?"

"Of course."

I snorted. "I didn't realize I needed a drink."

"You looked like you did. I can get you a regular ginger ale if you want, but I figured you might need the courage."

"It's what I needed." I took another gulp and set the glass down, picking up the water he had also handed me.

"Thank you," I whispered.

"The girls said you had the reading of the will today. I'm not going to ask if you're okay because, clearly, you're not. But do you want to talk about it?"

I nodded and told him exactly what had happened in the office. His eyes got marginally wider with each addition I made to the story.

"Holy shit," he whispered.

"Yeah. I wasn't expecting that. I don't know if I'll ever be in the right frame of mind to deal with everything that Grandma Sharon left me."

"That's a lot of responsibility. But, Myra? You're amazing. You can handle this. And you're not alone. We've got your back. The Brady brothers and the pact sisters. Always."

I wiped tears from my face, annoyed that I was crying again.

"One day, I will see you and not cry. I'm not a crier. I promise."

"A lot came at you recently." He paused. "Speaking

of. You really think your parents are going to contest the will?"

I nodded quickly. "I think they're going to do everything in their power to get to what my grandmother had. They didn't even let me come to the funeral. I definitely don't think they expected to hear what the lawyer had to say today."

"I don't know why not," Nate said, and I frowned. "Your grandmother used a lawyer from her old town, and everything's set up where you live now. They came out here, knowing that something was going to be weird. They had to expect something like this."

I shook my head. "I didn't."

"Because you're in shock over multiple things. They've had time to let it stew. They had to know some things wouldn't go exactly in their favor."

"I don't know if I quite believe that. But, either way, I think I'm officially disowned."

"I'm sorry."

I sighed and took another sip of my whiskey and ginger ale. "I don't think I can truly be sorry. I lost my family a long time ago. They kept pushing me out with each passing year. The way they looked at me today? I can't ever go back. Even though I don't know what of the past I would want to go back to."

"I understand. Well, I don't understand, because even though my parents don't live here, any time one of us ends up in the hospital for longer than a single treatment, they're right here."

"I hate that you guys keep ending up there."

He shook his head. "If our family could stop being shot at or stabbed, that would be great."

I winced. "Yes. I'm tired of visiting the hospital."

"I'm sorry you had to deal with everything you have. But you're through that step. And you're not alone."

"Do you want to go on a date with me?" I asked, surprising myself.

His eyes widened. "Are you asking because you're going through a lot and you're mourning right now? Because I don't want to take advantage of you."

I pressed my lips together before I let out a breath. "I have no idea what I'm doing, Nate. I feel like everything is slipping through my fingers like sand. But I'm tired of being afraid of what could happen and of what we lost. I can't forget the way you are, and how you're making me feel right now. Honestly, I'm just tired—of pushing, of fighting. We said we were going to start over. But I don't think I can ever be only friends with you, Nathan. And I think that was always the problem."

He stared at me for long enough that I squirmed, afraid I had said something stupid. That I'd pushed too hard or read the situation completely wrong.

He set down his glass, pulled mine from my hands, and tugged me to my feet.

"We were never going to be only friends, Myra. And that was the problem."

And then his lips were on mine, and I could forget —just for a moment. We might be using each other, but I didn't think it mattered.

Because I could get lost in him and the person he had been, as well as the man he was now.

And in his arms, I knew I wasn't alone.

If only for the moment.

Chapter 14

Nate

"When I accidentally asked you out on this date, I wasn't quite expecting this."

I snorted as I looked down at Myra, shaking my head. "Did you just say 'accidentally?'"

She shrugged, looking quite sexy in her little black getup as she pulled her hair back, tying it at the base of her skull.

"I didn't go to your house thinking that I was going to ask you out. It wasn't even on my mind. Even on the periphery. I simply blurted it out, and it felt right." She looked at me then, and I wanted to reach out and grab her, kiss her and tell her that everything was going to be okay—even if I wasn't quite sure I believed it.

"I'm delighted that you did, even though I have no idea if I would have asked you out. Mostly because we are excellent about never talking about the past."

I leaned down and pressed my lips firmly to hers before leaning back and handing over her paintball gun.

"Okay, we've done this once before, though it's been a few years. Do you need to relearn the basics?"

She shook her head and looked down at the weapon. "No, I remember. I'm not very good at it, but we'll have fun."

"Let's go over it again, just in case, as well as secure the rest of your protective gear. We'll be on the same team as a couple of people from my old job. And we're going up against the firefighters."

Her eyes widened. "Really? But aren't they, like, muscular and athletic?"

I snorted and let out a shocked gasp, taking a staggering step back. "Are you saying that I am not athletic or built?"

Her gaze raked me, and my dick hardened. "You do have your attributes."

"You keep talking about my attributes, and we won't be spending much time on the field."

"Okay, you two, that's enough of that," Ed said as

he came over. Ed had been my boss back when I was an EMT. He had retired early thanks to a back injury, an injury from the same accident I had been in, though he had lasted a couple of additional years behind the wheel. Eventually, he had given up, though, and now he spent his time at an at-risk youth center, working his ass off. That was how I'd heard about this place. He brought his kids here every once in a while, and the field was consistently maintained and supervised. I felt safe bringing Myra here, even though it never occurred to me that she would be the only girl here today.

"We're going over the rules and our game plan, and then we're going to beat those firefighter bastards."

"Am I the only civilian here?" Myra asked, glancing around, looking very cute in her helmet and getup.

Ed shook his head. "We're all civilians here, ma'am."

She raised a single brow. "Let's not call me ma'am."

Ed snorted and gave me a look.

"Just do what the lady says."

Ed grinned, making him look years younger. "I like you looking all whipped with that fishhook in your mouth."

"You're mixing metaphors," Myra said, her voice

cool, but I heard the laughter in her tone. And from the way the light in Ed's eyes danced, so did he.

"All of us are retired—if a bit early given our different ailments or wanting a career change. You're the only lady here, though. Not by choice," Ed added.

"So, you're not saying that a little lady should be scared of you?" she asked, and I sat back and let Ed deal with it. I kind of liked her all feisty and sounding like the old Myra instead of the one always yelling at me. It was nice for a change.

"We usually have a less dude-heavy crowd, but two of our usuals are pregnant, and therefore, can't be on the field. The other two are out of town. So…sorry, you're stuck with a bunch of testosterone."

Myra winked at me. "I think I can handle it."

"I sure hope so because we are on a winning streak when it comes to these guys. You can't be the reason we lose."

"No pressure," I said drily.

"You've been out of the game for the past two months, Brady. I needed to call your brother in as a ringer."

"Which one?" Myra asked.

"Technically, if they're not married into the group, they have to be in the medical field at least. So, Macon's the only one we can take."

"And it's okay that Nate and I aren't married?" Myra asked, her voice very careful.

It was weird to not stutter over the words, considering we had actually been married. But it didn't feel like that had been real. It was almost as if it were all a dream, and we were somehow coming out of the fog now.

We were finding our footing—only we weren't very good at it.

"No, you don't need the ring to be here. Now, let's go over the plan."

I slid next to Myra and tried my best not to reach out and grab her butt since it looked delicious in her black pants.

"Pay attention," Myra whispered.

"It's really hard."

Her gaze went to my crotch, and I snorted.

"That, too."

"Brady, do I need to split you two up?"

I shook my head. "No, sir. I'll pay attention."

"That's good. Just remember, I have stories from when you were a rookie. Every single late-night mistake and stupid thing you've ever done, I have them all right here." He tapped his temple. "I can tell Myra everything."

"I think you need to tell me everything anyway." Myra laughed, and everybody joined her.

"I made a terrible mistake in bringing you here," I said drily.

"Oh, no, this is going to be fun."

We broke into two by two groups as soon as the game started, and Myra and I crouched down low behind a fallen log. It was eight against eight, and whoever was left standing without paint on them won. It should be simple.

Except for the fact that I had shitty aim, and Myra was worse.

"My adrenaline is pumping," she whispered. "This is scary."

"We can quit if you want," I said quickly.

She shook her head. "No, I'm having fun, but it's sort of like when you're watching a TV show or a movie, and you're screaming at the girl to look behind her." She quickly looked over her shoulder, and I held back a laugh, and then did the same.

"All clear," I whispered.

"Good."

There was a crunch of leaves, and we ducked down, keeping quiet as two former firefighters walked past, their blue armbands signaling who they were. Myra and I had red bands, which I thought was hilarious considering firefighters should be red. But Ed had chosen the color for the Red Cross. So, in other words, the firemen could suck it.

Myra set up for the shot as I did, and I whispered under my breath. "Three, two, one." We both fired, and one of the men dove, both of us missing. Myra got her ball right on the other guy's chest, though. He cursed, looked towards us, and then threw his head back and laughed.

"Should have known it was you, Brady."

I didn't say anything, although Myra wanted to. I put my hand over her mouth and whispered in her ear.

"He's trying to find out where we are. We need to move."

She nodded, and we crawled away, laughing as paintballs soared over our heads.

We got two more, but then our luck ran out. We needed to cross over another fallen tree, but as we did, someone shouted, and Myra jerked. I heard the sound before it even came at us, and I tackled her to the ground, but it was too late. I cursed under my breath as three paintballs hit me in the side, right where Myra had stood. I rolled, keeping her out of harm's way. She pushed at me, cursing.

"Nate, I can handle it." She looked over her shoulder, shot twice, and the guy cursed.

"Great aim."

"And it seems we have a winner."

Ed came out over the ridge, and we all laughed, taking off our gear. Myra stood, looked at her very dirty yet perfectly black outfit, no spots of color, and did a little booty shake.

"Wow, talk about beginner's luck."

I narrowed my eyes at one of the single men who watched Myra's ass as she did her little dance, and he held up his hands, shaking his head.

"Looks like we need to celebrate," Ed said, and I raised a brow at the other man. "Next time. I do believe you have a date tonight."

Myra looked up at me, and I pressed my lips to hers.

"Congratulations, baby."

"I'm going to bruise, and you're going to have to suck up for the fact that you injured me."

I winced. "Sorry. But at least I'm going to have horrible welts from the paintballs."

"That is true. It will help me sleep at night."

The others laughed, and I pinched her ass. She squealed, and I pulled her away, the others laughing and planning our next outing.

As we cleaned up, piling everything into my truck, Myra grinned at me. "That was a blast."

"Really?" I asked and rubbed my temple.

"Are you okay?" she said.

"Yeah, I'm fine. Didn't hit my head or anything, but I think it was a little too much adrenaline for me. Do you mind driving home?"

She took the keys from me and kissed me softly.

"What was that for?" I asked.

"Because you aren't a big, tough guy who needs to drive the little lady around. As soon as your head started to hurt, you realized that maybe you might be getting a migraine, so you handed over your keys without a second thought. You asked for help."

"I had to learn the hard way that if I don't, I end up putting people I love in danger."

She frowned.

"I was the big, tough guy to Arden, even though she was having a good health day, and I wasn't. I ran a stop sign, and I almost killed us both. We were fine. I didn't even hit a curb or anything, but I threw up all over the interior of my car—and Arden. She's never let me live it down."

Myra winced. "That sounds horrible."

"It was. So now I take Ubers everywhere, or I have people drive me if I'm having a bad week driving. I've been fine recently, but this might have been a little too much for me."

"Oh, Nate. I'm sorry."

"Don't be. It was my idea, and I didn't know if it was going to be bad or not. I never do until I'm there. I don't take unnecessary risks. And that's why you're going to drive us home, so I'm not *your* unnecessary risk."

"Nate, I…" She trailed off, shaking her head.

I didn't know what she was going to say, and I was grateful she didn't finish the sentence.

Because in my head, it sounded so natural to say that I loved her right then. Because I did.

I fucking did.

I had wrapped that feeling around so much hate over the years that I hadn't let myself feel anything else.

But I loved her.

And I had no idea what the fuck to do about it.

We ended up picking up Thai on our way back to my place, and we retrieved Daisy from Macon's, as well.

"I love that Daisy doesn't have to spend the day at home alone and that she gets to spend time with her cousins."

I laughed. "Truth be told, I don't think the cats are all that happy she's there, but they're getting used to her."

"True. I guess since we're eating, she has to go back in the octagon?" Myra asked, setting down the food on the counter as I took Daisy out to the backyard to do her business.

"Yep. But we'll get her some food and water, and she'll be fine. As soon as she gets out of this chewing stage of hers, she can have a little more freedom. But according to Macon, it's one day at a time."

"You're a good puppy dad," Myra said as I brought Daisy back in, looking very proud of herself.

"I'm trying. Macon's the one with all the rules. I just do my best to follow them."

Myra looked down at herself and then grabbed her bag from the counter. "I'm going to shower and change. Do we need to stick the food in the fridge?"

"As long as you're not doing your hair or makeup or anything, I can at least set everything out and get it ready."

"That sounds like a plan. Because I'm starving."

I leaned over and took her lips with mine, groaning. "Me, too."

She pulled away, and I was thankful that she looked reluctant as her eyes darkened, and her cheeks reddened. And then she practically ran towards the bathroom.

We were moving far too fast for whatever this was.

It didn't feel real, and I knew she was still grieving. I knew we were figuring out what the hell we were going to do about who we were to each other.

But I didn't want to think about any of that just then. All I wanted to do was pretend for a minute.

And I was grateful that we were making that happen.

Myra came out wearing her well-worn jeans and a tee, her hair wet and piled on the top of her head.

"I usually only wear jeans for work. The fact that you are seeing them on me right now should tell you I wanted to be comfy, and these are my oldest pair of pants. Do not tell the rest of the world that I dared to go out in public not looking pristine."

I licked my lips and kissed her as I set the plates in front of her. "You always look fucking gorgeous to me."

"Is that a come-on?" she asked.

"If you have to ask, it wasn't a very good one. Will you bowl up the soup while I change?"

"I can do that. I'm starving."

"Once again, I'm going to say…me, too." I kissed her hard and then took the quickest shower of my life, putting on gray sweats and a white T-shirt even as I walked towards where she was. Daisy was asleep on her little bed, and I knew I'd have to take her out again soon. Myra sat on the floor near my coffee table, the food spread out before her, and an egg roll in her mouth.

"I couldn't wait," she said around her food.

I laughed, took a seat next to her so she was cradled between my legs and stole a bite of her egg roll. "Sounds good to me."

"Hey, that was mine!"

"What are you going to do about it?"

"Stop trying to sex me up when I'm eating. I'm starving."

"Okay, fine."

"No, not fine. You show up in your gray sweatpants, and I know you're not wearing any underwear because I can see your dick line."

My cock hardened even more, tenting my sweats. "You got a problem with that?"

"Start eating."

"You know what I want to eat."

"Nate."

And then I took her mouth, and she dropped the rest of the egg roll. We were on the other side of the table from the couch, so there was enough space, and I moved her to her back, kissing her softly.

"What are we doing?" She breathed into me.

"I don't know," I said honestly, afraid of what the answer might be.

"I don't want to think about it. We'll do this. No promises. Just you and me. No promises," she repeated.

I nodded, grateful. "You're right. For fun. No promises." Such a fucking lie. One that would break us both in the end.

"Okay, then kiss me."

And so I did. My hands slid up the back of her soft T-shirt, and I groaned.

"You're not wearing a bra."

"I couldn't help it. Everything felt so tight and too sensitive."

I crawled down her body and pushed her shirt up over her breasts. They fell heavily, and I lapped at her nipple, sucking one into my mouth and then letting it go with a pop. "Jesus Christ, you're beautiful."

"You always say the sweetest things."

"I'm not finished yet."

I moved to her other breast, giving it equal attention before pushing them together and licking and sucking, molding them with my hands. She moaned and arched into me, and I trailed my lips down her belly, nipping at her waist.

"Nate," she whispered.

I undid her jeans, and she arched her back and lifted her hips for me so I could pull them down and over her butt. I tugged the panties with them, and then she was mostly naked for me, her T-shirt pressed above her breasts, her pants and panties tangled in a pile next to us.

"I didn't get a chance to see you naked before. I'm so damn glad I get to look my fill right now. Although it may take me ages to get there."

"Stop looking and do something."

"You mean like this?" I asked and lowered my head to kiss her core. She arched against me, and I pressed her hips down, sucking, tasting. I spread her, licking her clit, and then delved deep inside her as she moaned, spreading her thighs even more. I slid one hand up and cupped her breast, playing with her nipple as I kept her open for me, tasting her sweetness and needing more. She moved, and I kept going, pleasuring her with my tongue and my mouth. And when she came, she angled more, pressing into my face, and I took over, sucking and tasting and needing.

She came down, and I hovered over her, kissing her, knowing that she could taste herself on my lips. The thought made me impossibly harder.

She tugged on my shirt and used her feet to pull at my sweatpants. I laughed and sat up, pushing off my clothes. My dick sprang free, slapping me on the stomach, and she reached out and pumped me.

"Wow," she whispered.

"Now that is the best compliment I've ever heard."

With the angles of our bodies, she was able to lean forward and lick the tip of my dick. I cursed, tangling my hand in her hair, the clip that held her hair up falling.

"You keep doing that, and I'm not going to last long."

"I'm fine with that," she said and swallowed a bit more.

I shook my head, even as my hips worked, fucking

her mouth. But then I pulled away, needing to be inside her.

"I need a condom," I whispered, my voice coming out in a heated rush.

"We both already proved that we were clean. And I'm on birth control. We don't need to go backwards."

My breath came out in a shudder, and I positioned myself at her entrance, keeping my gaze on hers.

"Jesus fucking Christ, I'm not going to last long," I breathed.

"Then get inside me."

And so I did, slowly teasing her entrance, then entering her a fraction of an inch at a time. She moaned, wrapping her legs around my waist and pulling me even deeper. When I was halfway there, I slammed home, forcing a groan out of both of us. There was no more need for words as we moved as one. When I rolled to my back, she knelt above me, rocking on my cock as she slid her hands over her breasts, pulling the rest of her shirt off and then riding me with abandon.

I leaned up, sucking one breast into my mouth, fucking her as she did the same to me. When she came, her mouth parted, and her eyes going impossibly dark, she squeezed me, forcing an orgasm out of me.

I gripped her hips, knowing I would likely leave bruises, but I squeezed and stayed inside her regardless, my dick twitching as I came, both of us shaking, our bodies sweat-slick.

We looked at each other, our food having gone cold, neither of us speaking.

I knew that was a fucking problem. Because we were pretending like the past hadn't happened, and yet it was something we were steeped in. It was why we were here in the first place.

This would probably blow up in our faces to the point where we would likely end up even more hurt than we already were.

But right then, with her around me, I didn't care.

I knew this was a mistake; every single time we touched and kissed and did something beyond talking and voicing our true feelings was.

But I didn't care.

Sadly, I knew it would be our downfall in the end.

Chapter 15

Myra

"I SWEAR PARKING GETS MORE RIDICULOUS EVERY year." Nate pulled in behind Cross's SUV.

I looked over my shoulder at Dakota, who rolled her eyes, and Macon rubbed his hand over his mouth. Joshua sat between them, the boy bouncing in his seat.

"I see the smirking. You may not be saying anything out loud, but I know you're judging me," Nate said as he turned off the car when he parked.

We all scrambled out of the vehicle, and I shook my head at him as we closed the doors.

"You sound a little more like a curmudgeonly old

man than usual," I laughed. He stalked over to me, twisted my hair in his hands ever so slightly, and kissed me hard on the mouth. The others made oohing and aahing sounds, and I pushed at him.

"Nathan."

"What? You called me curmudgeonly and old. I wanted to prove I'm not."

"What does curmudgeonly mean?" Joshua asked as he tugged on my hand.

I smiled. "It just means he's growly."

"Oh, then Dad gets curmudgeonly all the time," Joshua said, and my heart did that little extra twisting thing as I looked up at Macon and Dakota. Macon leaned down and kissed the top of Dakota's head, looking as proud as a peacock. Joshua was starting to call Macon "Dad" and did it as if he had been saying the phrase his entire life.

I was going to start crying any minute at the sweetness of it.

All of my friends had found their families, and I had, as well—only not in the same way.

I knew they were looking at Nathan and me as if we were ready for the next step, but I wasn't quite there yet. And I didn't think Nate was either. We were still trying to find our footing in the boggy ground that was our second time around when we hadn't even been aware that the first time had ended the way it had.

"Okay, are we all ready to go?" Hazel said, Cross, Paris, and Prior behind her.

"I think we are." I looked at the others, who nodded.

We were here for Music in the Foothills, a fun concert that raised money for local charities. It was an entertaining time for families—and great music in general. I had come the past two years, but this was my first time with a whole crew like this. It felt like I was part of a family, something bigger than myself. And I liked it. I had never done anything like this with my parents. This was far too informal with the food trucks and carts everywhere. People were camped out on blankets or in lawn chairs they had brought. It was usually very peaceful and a lot of fun. Kids ran around and played, and everybody had a good time.

It didn't get too rowdy, and you always felt safe when here. Plus, I got to be with people that I enjoyed being around, and that was all that mattered to me.

Nate slid an arm around me and kissed the top of my head. I frowned and looked up at him.

"What was that about?" I asked.

"You looked sad. I wanted to make you smile."

That little clutch came back, and I pushed it away and did my best to ignore it. I could not fall for Nate. I couldn't. Not the way I had before.

Before, it had been fast and hard and all-encompassing.

I had lost a part of myself because I hadn't known who I was. Now, I had a firmer grasp on who I was and who I wanted to be. I didn't know how Nate fit into that, or if he did at all. But that meant I had to remember exactly where I stood in my own reality before I let myself fall too quickly—or at all.

"I'm fine. I was thinking about the fact that my parents would never be caught dead here."

Nate snorted. "Oh, hell no. Not even in the slightest. Although I'd like to see your mom try to sit down on a picnic blanket with one of those tight skirts she wears."

I raised a brow. "Okay, gross. You noticed how tight my mother's skirts are?"

He blushed and shook his head. "No, but it looks like she's always standing too straight in those pencil skirts. Like it's hard to move around. Very uptight with a stick up her ass." He paused. "Sorry. I shouldn't be so rude."

"No, no. I agree with you. Mom always has a stick up her ass. And yes, she'd never demean herself by sitting down on a blanket with the common folk."

"Okay, I'm sorry for bringing them up."

I shook my head. "I'm the one who thought about them and first mentioned them. All you did was make a weird comment about my mother's skirts."

"Please, let's never mention this again. Not if I want to sleep with you."

I laughed. "Yes. If you ever want sex again, then you can't talk about my mother."

"That sounds like a deal to me."

"What are you guys talking about?" Joshua asked, sliding between us. He took our hands, and I looked down at the boy. Once again, I felt a little tug.

I looked up at Nate, and he had an odd expression on his face that I knew likely mirrored mine.

If we hadn't been pulled apart, would we have a boy around Joshua's age? Would we have a child of our own who held our hands and called Nate Daddy?

There was no use dwelling on the past, not when it had stood in our way for so long already.

But it didn't make it any easier to forget.

Nate cleared his throat, and his expression went back to the fun uncle, and not the one with memories that haunted us both. He was so much better at this than I was. I defaulted to icy bitch queen, but he went to the nice guy.

We were both good at hiding things. It was no wonder we had never known the truth of ourselves before now.

Nate grinned. "We were just thinking about how much funnel cake we're going to eat."

"I've never had a funnel cake. Is it good?" Joshua

asked.

I pressed my lips together and raised a brow at Nate.

"I think it's time we gorge ourselves on funnel cake."

"I don't know if Dakota will like that," I sing-songed.

"What is Dakota not going to like?" the woman in question asked as she came up to my side and hooked her arm with mine.

"We're discussing funnel cake."

Dakota cringed. "Really, Nate?"

"Don't blame Nate," Macon put in. "I was going to get one for us anyway."

"It's so much grease and sugar," Dakota said.

"Did you say sugar?" Joshua asked, bouncing on his toes. I laughed, then let go of his hand to run my fingers through his hair.

I shook my head. "We'll make sure you get all the funnel cake and horrible junk food you could ever want. But you're not allowed to puke."

We stood in line, waiting to get into the venue, and Joshua looked up at me, his eyes wide.

"I'm going to puke? Cool."

I rolled my eyes. "No. You're not allowed to puke. We will be the fun aunts and uncles who give you junk food, but only on special occasions because your mother will disown us if we go too far. However, you're not allowed to puke. I despise vomit."

"Okay. I promise not to puke. In front of you."

That made me laugh, and Nate grinned and gave the little boy a high-five. "Seriously, though, I puked in front of Myra once, and she threw up right next to me. Spewed everywhere."

"Do not tell him that story," I chided, and everybody laughed.

"Oh, but you need to tell us," Prior said on a laugh.

"It was nothing. It was in college. Things happen. We are not telling everybody that story. I'm a sympathetic vomiter. Even talking about it…" I took a deep breath and swallowed the bile in my throat. "Okay, now I don't want a funnel cake. Look at what you've done. You have ruined junk food for me."

"Not all of it will be junk food," Macon said, shaking his head. "I see a couple of food trucks down there that have been in the downtown area near my practice. That taco truck? It's gourmet."

"Ooh." I eyed the vehicle.

"Oh, yes, there's a bunch of fusion trucks around here," Dakota added.

"Okay, so you guys get the funnel cake and we can gorge ourselves on gourmet," Hazel said, looking down at her notes. Why she had a notebook—as did Paris—I'd never know.

"I think we need to get one of everything." Cross rubbed his hands together.

"Yes, everybody's going to have a bite of everything they want, but I promise, nobody's going to puke." Hazel met my gaze.

I visibly shuddered. "Okay, that's enough of that." I turned to change the subject. "I'm sorry that Arden couldn't come." I glanced between the brothers.

"The last time we came here, the sun was a bit too much for her. It flared her lupus," Nate explained. "She's hanging out with Liam and his family today since a few of them aren't feeling well."

My brows rose. "What do you mean?"

"I'm pretty sure it's morning sickness," Cross said, grinning like a fool.

"Oh my gosh, how many of them are pregnant?" I asked.

"I'm not sure, but I think they're enjoying themselves. Since we're still waiting to hear about the adoption process for Liam and Arden, they have a lot of plans to go through. So, they're just hanging out today, and we've got the rest of the Bradys here at the music festival."

"Yay, I love that we're all Bradys." Joshua skipped with Macon as we passed the line, and I gave everyone a bright smile, trying to ignore the awkward tension.

The rest of them were Bradys. I wasn't even an ex, technically. I hadn't taken Nate's last name.

And I wasn't engaged or married to him now.

I wasn't a Brady.

And I didn't know if I wanted to be.

We made our way to an open section of the park where we could lay out our large blankets, claiming our territory. There was the main stage, but we didn't need to get too close to be able to hear anything. Everyone else could get closer and be bunched together. We liked our space, and with the screens and speakers, you weren't missing anything if you were a little farther away.

"Okay, I'm heading off to start the first food run."

"I'm with you," Nate added.

"We'll all take turns, but we should have at least more than one person, given the amount of land," Paris said, looking out at the rest of our area like a drill sergeant.

Cross smiled. "We've got it."

"Oh yes, you do. Now, come and take these," Hazel ordered. "I've made a list."

I groaned. "Really? A list of the food we need?"

"A list of places to go. I already looked up many of the trucks, so we should be able to get to them before it gets too busy. And this way, we at least get the food we want, and maybe find a few surprises along the way.

Dakota, Macon, and Joshua can hang out here. I will bring food to them like they're Roman gods."

"I like the sound of that," Dakota said, leaning against Macon as Joshua ran around the two of them, laughing.

"Okay then, troops. Let's head out."

Nate put his hand in mine, and we made our way to the funnel cake area.

"Really? We get stuck with the funnel cakes?"

"To start. At least so Joshua can taste it. We're not going with dessert after everything. This is going to be fun. And probably gross."

"Sounds like a plan."

It was a bit crowded, so we were jostled a bit, but when someone ran right into me, their shoulder digging into mine, and their elbow piercing, I tripped and pressed into Nate, trying not to fall flat on my face.

He frowned and righted me since I had nearly fallen.

"Are you okay? What the hell?"

I rubbed my shoulder and my side, looking around. "I could have sworn that was Roland." I shook my head. "It wasn't. It can't be. Why would he be here?"

"Are you sure it wasn't your cousin? You said he was angry."

I frowned, shaking my head again. "No. It wasn't him. Just a man with dark hair. It surprised me, I guess, and I put Roland's face on everybody I'm angry at lately."

"I'm glad it's not me these days," Nate said dryly, and I knew he said it to cut the tension, but I was still worried.

I looked over my shoulder again, rubbing my side. "That did hurt."

"Do you need to go to the med-tech tent to have it checked out? Or do you need to go home? Want me to look?"

"No, I'm fine. Nothing a funnel cake can't fix."

Nate searched my face and then pinched my chin before kissing me softly. "I'll get you anything you want, Myra. All you need to do is ask."

I swallowed hard and held back a smile.

That was the problem, wasn't it? He would do anything I asked now.

But what if I didn't know what I wanted?

We got our funnel cake and a couple of other things on the list to the point where our hands were full, and we were laughing. The food smelled amazing. Nothing was too junky here. Everything was perfect. We made our way back to the blankets at the same time as everybody else, and soon, we were tasting beer, eating tacos and teriyaki chicken on a stick, and inhaling funnel cakes and falafels and other random things we had picked up.

"I'm stuffed," I said, leaning against Nate's back. Everybody was sprawled on top of one another, looking like deities after a feast. Nate kissed my temple before eating another bite of a new funnel cake. I laughed, looking down at my hair, knowing I had powdered sugar everywhere.

"For the love of God, if ants find me and dig their way into my hair, I will never forgive you."

"Now that's an image that I'm never going to be able to get out of my mind," Paris said dryly. She looked over at us and shook her head. "First of all, you two are too cute. Second, Nate, clean up your woman. Don't throw sugar all over her."

"Should I make a joke about how she's already sweet enough?" he asked, and I groaned, closing my eyes.

"That was ridiculous."

I saw the questioning glances, and I knew that nobody would ask outright.

Are they serious? What exactly is going on? Does she love him? Does he love her?

Those were all very good questions, ones that I was not going to address because I didn't want to know the answers.

We needed to go slower than we had before. And that was the problem. There was always *the before* when it came to Nate and me.

I didn't know if I could love him again. Or let myself acknowledge that I maybe already did.

Or remember that I always had.

And that was the problem. I had never truly fallen *out* of love with Nate.

I hadn't let myself say the words, but they had always been there in the back of my mind. Waiting. Lurking. Whenever I went on a date with someone else or caught my reflection in the mirror, thinking of something happy about my future, Nate was there.

And now, he was *here*, wrapped around me, his family surrounding us as we listened to music and enjoyed ourselves.

There was no going back from this. If I broke again, I would have to walk away. And I didn't know if I was strong enough to do that.

It might be smarter for us to walk away now, to go back to only being friends or at least trying to be—with nothing else in between.

Or perhaps it'd be better if I just walked away entirely. Cut ties. No one would be hurt.

I didn't know the right answers. All I knew was that if Nate left again, or pushed me away, I wasn't sure I'd be strong enough to pick up the pieces.

And the worst part was, I didn't know if I had picked them up from before when he shattered me the first time.

Chapter 16

Nate

I was falling in love with my ex-wife. And why did that sound like I was living in a country song?

Maybe because I *was* living a country song.

I couldn't fall for Myra. Not this fast. Not this hard. Not again.

But here we were, weeks into being together. Weeks into staying with each other nearly every night and day. Weeks into me bringing Daisy over to her house so I could work in her living room while she was in her studio, so we could be close. Weeks into her coming to sketch while Daisy crawled all over her, and I worked on my latest project.

All those weeks, and we had fallen right back into one another. It should've been a problem. It *was* a problem. But I didn't want it to be one. I didn't want to fall as hard as I was. But here I was, and there was no going back—a phrase I told myself often. Because I was falling for my ex-wife. For Myra. And I didn't think she would ever be able to fall for me again.

Despite the fact that she spent so much time with me. Or that we were becoming friends again and being better about who we were, I didn't think she could truly forgive me for what I did. I might not have made the photos. I might not have forced her hand. But I *had* broken her trust and her heart and hadn't believed her.

And I didn't know how to change that.

"Hey there," Myra said as she walked into the house, and dropped to her knees.

In a perfect world, she'd be falling to her knees for something a little more fun. Instead, she grinned and hugged Daisy to her. The puppy wiggled her little butt and lapped at Myra's chin, while the woman I loved laughed back and pushed our dog down ever so slightly.

And I had just called Daisy, *our* dog. I hadn't meant to, even in my head, and I would do my best not to say that out loud. Myra would end up running faster than ever before if I said something along those lines aloud.

I needed to be better. I had to stop focusing on what we used to have and what we could have and focus on what we *did* have. But that wasn't going to be easy.

"Hello there. I'm here, too," I said, mock-pouting.

"I'm sorry." Myra laughed. "It's so good to see you, Nate. Now, I need to go back to loving this puppy with all of my heart. Who's my precious baby?" Myra said before getting a chew toy and playing with Daisy around the living room.

"You know you're getting a little ridiculous with my dog."

"I can't help it. She loves me more."

I love you, too.

Jesus Christ, I needed to not think those words. Because if I did, I would end up saying them out loud. And Myra would run faster than a coyote chasing a roadrunner.

"So, I ordered in. I hope that's okay."

Myra looked up and smiled. "It's fine. Long project today?"

I nodded, rubbing the back of my neck. "Yes, it's bugging me because I don't think it's what I need to write. I think it's just me."

"Headaches?" she asked, standing up to come up to me. She put her hands on my chest, kissed me softly, and then stared into my eyes. I knew she was searching for pain markers. And she would probably find them. She frowned again and then reached up to rub my temples. I practically moved into her like a cat wanting to be petted, but I held back any purring or groaning.

Barely.

"I could've cooked for you," she said, and I shook my head, pushing her hair behind her ear.

"No, you didn't need to. I ordered from our favorite fusion place. So, we're about to get bulgogi and teriyaki and love it."

"You know that's our favorite place because we like the sushi," she said dryly.

"True, but I can't do delivered sushi. I know it can be amazing, but it's weird for me."

She snorted. "Yes, it's much better than gas station sushi, but I am particular, as well. Why don't you sit down? I'll rub your neck while you play with Daisy."

"You know, that sounds quite nice."

"Good, because…get on the floor."

I raised a brow. "Ordering me around?"

"Always. You know that Daisy's not allowed on the furniture until she's a year old, and since you're going to cuddle her, you need to be on the floor, too."

"I still don't understand why she can't be up there, but Macon told me not to, and therefore, here we are."

"You are always going to listen to what the vet tells us about your precious baby girl."

I kissed her hard and then sank to the floor, nipping at her hip as I did.

She moaned but narrowed her eyes at me. "Behave."

"What if I don't want to?" I asked and winked.

Daisy, excited that I was sitting with her, barked, wiggled her butt, and then brought me her favorite stuffed cow, Moo Moo. "Thank you," I said, and Daisy plopped onto my lap and promptly fell asleep.

Myra sat behind me and began rubbing my shoulders. I leaned into her, the puppy snoring on my lap, and felt like I could do this forever. Like this was *it*—everything I'd ever wanted.

"Feel better?" she asked, her voice low.

"Mmm. Thank you."

"I hate that you have headaches. That I can't help beyond this."

I looked up at her, then took her hand and kissed her palm. She gave me a small smile, and it felt like the best thing in the world. "You being here? It's better than anything else you could've done. Usually, I deal with these things alone—or now, with Daisy. But I like you being here in my space, next to me. Helping me."

I wanted to say more, but I knew if I did, it would be a mistake. Too much, too fast. Thankfully, the doorbell rang.

"I'll get it." Myra wiggled around me so she could get up.

"I already paid," I called out.

"Okay," she said, and I shook my head.

I knew Myra had way more money than I did. She would always have more. It wasn't a problem for me, though, and I didn't mind that she sometimes paid for us to go out. However, she occasionally got a little affronted over the idea that I wanted to pay.

It was just a thing, though. We would alternate like any couple good at finding balance.

Only I didn't know what that would be for us.

"It smells delicious." Myra walked into the living room. I stood up, Daisy in my arms, and then took her outside to take care of her business. After, I put her in her octagon, where she promptly fell back asleep.

"She already ate dinner. Now, it's time for us."

Myra's eyes darkened, and I kissed her again. "Food first," she said. "I'm starving."

"It's like you knew exactly where my mind was going," I laughed.

"I always know where your mind is going, Nathan Brady."

"I am sweet and innocent. I have no idea what you mean."

Myra snorted and sat down next to me, leaning between my legs as the two of us divvied up our food, plates piled high with bulgogi and broccoli and teriyaki chicken.

"This smells so good," Myra repeated. "Either that, or the fact that I skipped lunch probably makes me think everything smells amazing."

I frowned. "You skipped lunch?"

"Yes. I was stressed out over a simple phone call, and it took me forever to get into my project. But then I was in the middle of it, and I was having a good day after that. In the zone. Lots of painting."

"What phone call?" I asked, tapping her lip with my fork. She opened, and I slid the chicken inside. She frowned.

"I can feed myself."

"It's hotter when I feed you."

"You say that, but now there's teriyaki on my chin, isn't there?"

She narrowed her eyes, and I shrugged and reached for the napkin to clean her up.

"There. All gone."

"But now I'm all sticky," she said, and I groaned.

"Stop saying random sexy things to distract me. What was the phone call about?"

"I just said I was sticky. That's not sexy."

"Do I need to make you sticky so you could see how sexy it is?" I asked, raising a single brow.

"Okay, okay, fine. Later."

"Phone call."

She sighed. "It was my parents' lawyer. I think they're going to contest the will completely. They were giving me one last chance or something like that. It's ridiculous."

Rage spiraled through me, and I took a deep breath so I didn't take it out on Myra. "What do they think you did? Conspired with your grandmother to steal money that wasn't even theirs to begin with?"

"I have no idea. And it doesn't matter. It's going to be a lot of work to deal with this entire estate. I'm starting to think my grandma didn't even like me if she forced me to deal with all this on my own."

I shook my head and took her hand in mine. "She knew you could handle it. And you have people to lean on if you need to."

"I should be able to do it myself."

"Myra, we both know you don't have to."

"I'm just used to doing things that way. I always have. Even before I met you, Nate. I've always been alone when it comes to my family."

I didn't know what to say to that. I wanted to tell her that I would always be here for her, that her friends and I would be here. But I couldn't promise that. Not when I was afraid she would push me away if I got too close, too quickly.

"What can I do?" I asked.

"Nothing yet. I don't think my grandmother trusted anybody else to take care of all of this. She gave Lacey a lot for her children, and there's responsibility in that, but there are so many other things. My lawyer's helping me with it, but we're at a standstill at the moment while we wait to see what my family's going to do."

"I hate this for you."

"It's not my favorite thing. And it completely derailed me this morning. So, when I finally got in the mood to paint and work on the project for the commission I need to be paid for, I skipped lunch. That's why I'm starving now. But the food is good. Even if you got me all sticky."

She winked, and I laughed like she likely intended.

"I'm not the greatest with investments and estates and things like that, but you know Arden's husband, Liam, is. He deals with a bunch."

"Because he's a multi-millionaire, former famous model, and now a bestselling author?" she asked.

"I don't know if you have to sound so excited about all those things."

She snorted. "I had such a crush on him when I was younger. Liam is very handsome."

"So I hear. Too bad he's already married to my baby sister."

"To your twin. I was only ribbing you. He may be handsome, but he's taken."

"And?"

"And I guess I have you. So, yeah, I can't have him."

"You know, I'm about to throw this rice in your face," I growled.

"You wouldn't dare."

I looked at the rice, and then at her, and shook my head. "No, because I'm hungry. You're lucky I didn't eat enough for lunch either. Hence, the headache."

"Okay, I guess I should feed you." She pressed the fork full of bulgogi to my lips, and I slid it off the tines with my tongue, my gaze on her.

"Who knew bulgogi could be so sexy?" she purred.

I laughed and nearly choked on my beer as I took a sip. "Thank you for that," I said.

"Should you be having a beer with a headache?" she asked.

I shook my head. "Probably not, but here we are."

We finished our food, checked on Daisy, and then brought everything to the kitchen to clean up.

"I seriously have bulgogi on my face and my hands.

Feeding each other and being sexy with this kind of food probably wasn't the best idea." She laughed.

"It looks like I need to clean you up." I kissed her hard, swiping my tongue over hers. She moaned.

"Seriously, it's everywhere. I think you got bulgogi in my bra." Myra laughed again.

"I would never dare waste good quality beef like that. However, I guess you're going to have to take your bra off so I can check."

She snorted and shook her head. "Seriously, though, what do you say we take a shower?"

My dick hardened, pressing against my zipper. I nodded quickly. "Okay, let's go." I turned around, slapped her on the ass, and pushed her forward. "Strip off those clothes, baby. Let's get in the shower."

"Eager much?"

"My dick has been hard since you rubbed against it earlier, and now I'm pretty sure I'm going to have a zipper scar for the rest of my life."

"Aw, poor baby. You're going to have to take your pants off so I can see, though, just to check."

I laughed and stripped off my shirt as we made our way into the bathroom.

We laughed, kissing, letting our hands trail over each other as we quickly stripped off our clothes and stood in my tall shower. I had a bench seat that I used whenever I had a severe headache, one of the upgrades I had put in when Arden said that I needed to take better care of myself.

And now, I was fucking grateful for it.

"Sit," I said as I turned on the warm water. The water slicked over my back and misted over Myra as she spread her legs on the bench. I dropped to my knees in front of her and lapped.

"Damn," she muttered, her hands pressing against the glass on either side of us. "This isn't good for water," she moaned.

"Then I'll have to be fast," I whispered against her and then spread her before licking her clit. I speared her with two fingers as I kissed her harder, and she shuddered, her whole body shaking against me. When she came, her legs wrapped around my neck and she pressed into me, her entire body blushing under my attentions and from the water.

I moved away so she could lean down and capture my lips.

"I taste myself," she whispered.

"You're so fucking hot," I muttered. "So fucking… everything," I whispered, not sure what else I should or could say. I couldn't even think.

Instead, I kissed her again, my hands roaming over her breasts and her hips as she sat in front of me. I knelt between her legs until she tugged me up. I stood, and her lips were suddenly around my cock.

I let my head fall back, the water sliding over our bodies as she took me in hand and hollowed her cheeks. She hummed along my length and bobbed her head, taking me in whole as she cupped my balls.

"I'm not going to last long," I muttered.

She didn't say anything. Instead, she sucked in her cheeks and kept going as my back tingled, and my balls tightened. I moved back, pulling her hair ever so slightly so she let go.

"I need you," I whispered. She stood up and pressed her breasts to my chest as I kissed her hard, both of us sliding against one another. I turned her in my arms, and she placed her hands on the glass. I gripped her hips and spread her cheeks.

"One day, I'm going to want this ass of yours," I muttered, pressing my thumb to her.

She shuddered, pushing back into me.

I played with her a bit, and she wiggled.

"Maybe, but only for you."

"Jesus Christ, don't tempt me like that."

"Then start fucking me, Brady."

"As my lady commands," I said and spread her again before I thrust into her in one stroke.

We both froze, her body stretching to accommodate me as my dick twitched.

I let out a breath, then pulled out again before pressing forward. I slid one hand up, cupping her breast as I fucked her from behind, both of us panting with need.

But this wasn't only fucking. It was so much more. This was the woman I knew inside and out. I could imagine doing this for the rest of my life.

I wanted this for the rest of my life.

And I was so fucking afraid that I wouldn't get it.

She moaned and pressed her back to my front. I latched on to her neck, my hands sliding over her wet body as we moved as one, arching into each other.

When she came again, her inner walls clamping around my cock, I pressed my fingers over her clit. I got impossibly harder, both of us panting, no words needed. And then I came, filling her, the bliss a perfect cacophony of both silence and madness.

We fought to catch our breath, and then I pulled out, turning her in my arms so I could kiss her, the water moving over us and bringing us even closer together.

"That was amazing," she whispered.

"And I'm not even done yet."

And I wasn't. I didn't think I would ever be done with Myra.

Because all I wanted to do was tell her how I felt, what I needed, what I thought I could give her. Only I still didn't think I was enough for her.

I didn't say anything, simply captured her lips with

mine and did the only thing I could. I cared for her. I washed her hair and her body. I took care of the woman I loved.

And I hoped to hell that she'd forgive me enough to love me back someday.

Chapter 17

Myra

"This one's stunning," Arden said from my side as she went over one of my canvases in my studio.

I took a step toward her and smiled. "This is one of my favorites. I painted it rather quickly, the idea coming to me after a rainstorm." I paused. "That sounds wishy-washy."

Arden met my gaze and shook her head. "It sounds how you need it to be. There's nothing wrong with finding inspiration in things around you. Not to mention, it's a beautiful piece. It's far more abstract than your others, but I like it."

I nodded. "Sometimes, I just want to see the mood rather than a portrait or landscape. It all depends on what I'm looking at when I decide I need to paint."

"I think this one might be my favorite. I can't decide. And the fact that I can't tells me this was a perfect idea. Thank you so much for letting me shop in your studio for Liam."

"Thank you for wanting a piece for *the* Liam Montgomery."

Arden snorted. "Oh, yes, make sure you tell my husband that to his face. I don't think his ego is quite big enough yet."

I laughed. "I'm sure you've stroked his ego as much as needed." I paused. "You know, if Nate or Liam or any of the other guys were here, or even Paris for that matter, they'd probably make a stroking joke."

"The fact that you said that at all pretty much makes the reference for itself," Arden said primly, and then we both broke out into laughter.

"Seriously, thank you. I've been trying so hard to think of what to get Liam for his birthday, but the man has everything that he could ever want."

"I know what you mean. Nate's birthday's coming up, and I can't decide what to get him. He doesn't want much, and when he does, he buys it for himself. Then I have to be creative, and I'm like, do I want to get him a painting when it's my work rather than something fun?"

"It can be both, but I completely understand. Do you let others shop in your studio often?" she asked, taking a look at a landscape I had painted the year before.

"No, not really. Or ever. I paint pieces for the girls individually, but you're the first to shop in my studio when it doesn't have to do with an art show."

Arden froze, and looked over at me, smiling big. "Wow, I'm doubly honored. Thank you." She paused. "Why are you letting me?"

I shrugged and looked over the pieces. "Because you're Nate's twin, and because I like you."

Arden smiled wider, her eyes going kinder if that was even possible. "That's sweet. I love that you and Nate are back together," she said suddenly, and I froze.

"It feels weird sometimes to think that we are," I said, not knowing what else to say.

"We haven't had a chance to talk since the two of you got back together."

I looked around the room, memories flooding in of the time before. "There isn't much to talk about."

Arden snorted. "Okay, well, that was a complete lie."

I grimaced. "A complete lie." I sighed.

I didn't know what else to say.

"It was odd not telling everybody what had happened between the two of you so many years ago. It wasn't my place to say anything, and I never did."

I looked at her and met her gaze. "I'm sorry for putting you in that position. You didn't deserve that stress."

"It didn't stress me out. It didn't hurt me at all. But I hated the idea that either of you was in pain. Because while I know my brother unequivocally believed what he saw in those photos, it didn't make sense that you would do that to him."

I pushed back tears and nodded. "Thank you for saying that."

"He understood, too. That's probably why he was so blindsided. Why it hurt so much."

"Perhaps. I'm still so upset with my parents for doing such a thing."

"I'd be upset, too. Probably more than a little. As it was, I hated you right alongside Nate for a while until I realized it wasn't my place to cast judgment on anyone."

Pain ricocheted through me, but I nodded tightly. "You thought I had hurt your brother. Your twin. I'd probably have hated me, too."

"And that would have been wrong. It *was* wrong. All because your parents wanted something for themselves." She paused. "Something I hear is still the case."

I rubbed my hands over my thighs and gestured for her to join me in my little seating area in my studio. We plopped down on my comfortable couch, and I groaned. "I don't understand them. My parents are well-off. Far more than I am."

"And yet, they want more. Maybe they merely want the power that comes from knowing they can lord things over you. But now, you have that power in your hands. You've taken something from them, at least in their mind, and it shifted the dynamic."

I rubbed my temples. "Either way, it's a mess. And, eventually, I'm going to have to deal with it. Probably in court or in person. There's only so much I can do through my lawyer."

"Try not to let them get to you."

"I don't know what to do."

"As long as they don't push their way into your life and break what you have, you're going to come out the other side stronger."

I looked at Nate's sister and smiled. "I hope that's the case. I hope we can all push this behind us and move on and into whatever our future needs to be."

Arden opened her mouth to say something and then shook her head.

"What?" I asked.

"That seemed like the perfect segue to ask what your intentions are with my brother and how you're feeling. But then I realized that sounded too much like prying. So, never mind."

I blew out a breath. "I don't have answers for you. I wish I did, but I need some time."

"And neither of you took any time before. I'm glad you are now. I love my brother, and you're part of our family now, Myra, even if it's not through Nate. You're our friend. We have a connection. And we don't want you to get hurt either."

I pressed my lips together and nodded before standing up to stretch my back. "Let's look at that painting again for Liam, and we can come up with a plan."

"As long as you charge me full price," Arden said, nodding at me. "No family discount."

"Oh, there's going to be a family discount, didn't you just say I was connected?" I tried to sound light, as if I didn't have a care in the world. But she saw right through that, and I didn't blame her.

I didn't know what I felt for or about Nate, and I wasn't good at hiding that I was lost.

And Arden saw right through it.

We made a plan for Liam. I would drop off the painting at his birthday party, rather than Arden taking it now and hiding it from him. I didn't mind, and I thought it would look perfect in their home, picturing where it would be in Liam's office.

I figured I could go back to work, or maybe I should read a book or rest my brain for a bit. My mind was going in a thousand different directions, and it was hard for me to focus on anything. And it didn't help that I kept thinking about Nate and what our future could be.

I was so scared. *So* scared to want to feel and to be. So, I wouldn't.

This was a momentary place in time.

Eventually, we would walk away and be friends. However, the sooner we did that, the easier it would be—and the less pain there would be in the end.

The doorbell rang, and I frowned, trying to figure out who it could be. Honestly, it could be anyone since everybody kept trying to see what was up with Nate and me; they constantly stopped by.

I shook my head, a smile playing on my face as I opened the door, only to frown as soon as I saw who was there.

"Mother."

My mother stormed in, not even bothering to ask to be allowed inside. Her high heels clicked on my hardwood as she spun and narrowed her eyes.

The house was the same as it had been before.

Cleaner even since my ladies had already been through to help me with any dust and vacuuming.

My mother hated the place, that was clear, and that made me love it even more.

There was probably something wrong with me.

"Why don't you come right in?" I asked, trying to keep my voice from going too cold. I knew I was failing.

"You need to stop whatever you're doing."

I shook my head. "I'm not doing anything, Mother. I'm simply trying to live my life."

"You are stealing from your family."

I took a step back and shook my head. "How could I possibly be stealing from the family? I rarely talk to you. I have nothing to do with you."

"And yet, my mother's seen fit to give you everything. What did she see in you?" Her gaze traveled the length of my body, a look of distaste covering her features.

I tried not to let the slight hurt, the idea that my mother wanted nothing to do with me, and all she saw was what was lacking. But I couldn't let it do too much.

Not when everything hurt already to begin with.

"You need to go. We're already talking through our lawyers. Let's continue doing that."

My mother snarled. "You think it's so easy? To walk away and think you get everything. I don't know what you did to *my* mother, but I will never forgive you for daring to take what is not yours."

"You need to leave. I loved Grandma. I wish I could have convinced her to come out here. To be in a place she loved. But in the end, she wanted to be where she lost her husband. Your father. And I understood that. But I didn't convince Grandma to do anything. I never expected anything from her but her love. And I didn't even get a chance to say goodbye. You took that away from me."

"Stop it. I took nothing from you. You're the one daring to take from us."

"That's a lie, and you know it."

"You are going to regret this. Believe me."

She stormed past me and went to my front door. "We're officially contesting the will. I gave you your last chance. You'll be sorry." And then she blew out of my house, leaving me standing there, wondering how the hell I had come from that woman.

My hands shook, and I wanted to call Nate, to have him tell me that everything would be okay and hold me.

But I didn't.

That would be leaning on him too much. And I wasn't ready for that. I needed to remain cold and distant. If I relied on anyone too much, it would only hurt when things broke later.

So, I let out a breath and called my cousin. Lacey picked up after the first ring. "Hey there. How are you?"

Tears pricked the backs of my eyes, but I ignored them. They wouldn't help anyone. "My mother was just here. They're officially contesting the will. It might hurt the trust for your kids, as well."

Lacey cursed under her breath, very imaginative utterances that I would have to write down for later.

"Are you okay? Do you need me to drive down there?"

Tears once again threatened.

"I'm okay. She's said worse things to me."

Lacey paused long enough that I was afraid I had said too much.

"Just because you're used to her attitude and the way she treats you doesn't make it right."

"Perhaps. But I can't change her. I can only try to be myself."

"That sounds perfect to me, and very much like something Grandma would say. If you need me, I'm here. And my husband's family and I can take care of my children. We always have. Grandma Sharon's extra little bump would have been a nice way to secure their futures, but we can take care of our own if your parents and Roland ruin everything."

"It might be the other cousins, too. Not only Roland."

"Oh, I know. You were always the sane one of the bunch."

I smiled. "Funny, I used to think that about you."

"I'm here if you need me. I might bring the whole family down to bug you for a meal one day. We live so close now. We need to be a family."

My heart warmed, surprising me that it could after such a horrendous evening. "You're right. We do need to be a family. And I'm glad you're close."

"You know, Grandma was the one who pushed me to marry the man I love. To take that leap and to move out here. She gave me all the guidance I needed."

"I didn't know that."

"It seems there are a lot of things we don't know about each other. Let's figure them out."

We talked for a few more minutes, and I already felt lighter as we hung up. We would make plans to meet up and have a meal. I wanted to see her children, meet the family she had made on her own.

Lacey seemed well adjusted and as if she had made a good life for herself.

Maybe I could do that someday, but I wasn't sure that's what I was made for.

Lacey's mother wasn't as cruel as mine, after all.

And Lacey hadn't been broken because of lies and deceit.

I pushed those thoughts from my head and went back to my studio. I would relax later. Maybe I could put whatever I was feeling into my painting. Or I could simply forget.

My phone dinged, and I looked down, seeing a text from Nate.

Nate: *Thinking of you. Have a good night, babe.*

I didn't smile. I didn't do anything. I only remembered the hurt of when I'd walked away before, when my parents had ruined everything.

They had broken Nate and me before, and my mother had threatened us again.

What would they do this time?

And what would we believe?

I put away my phone and went back to work, telling myself that I would call him later. That I would pretend that everything was okay.

But that was my fear, that I was only pretending.

What would happen when reality crashed in, and I had to face what was there, and what clearly wasn't?

Chapter 18

Nate

I STOOD IN THE STUDIO, LOOKING AROUND AT THE ART pieces, my heart racing. "I knew you were talented, baby, but I didn't know you had this in you. I should have, but wow, I'm speechless."

Myra blushed, even though she had her back straight, the rest of her unflappable, but that little blush told me I'd connected to something.

And, damn it, that's what I'd wanted to do.

"I'm glad you feel that way, because my art show is coming up soon. I'd better have a good basis for what needs to go on those bare walls."

I shook my head and took a couple of steps towards her. I cupped her face and met her gaze. "There's enough talent in your little pinky finger to take my breath away. I'm honored that you showed me these before you showed your agent."

She shrugged, her eyes downcast.

She had done that a lot over the past week. Pulling away slightly as if everything was a bit too much for her. I didn't know why. We had been doing well—at least I'd thought. But she had been pulling away ever so slightly, and I didn't know how to make her stop.

"Anyway, I have eighteen pieces, but they want twenty. I can't decide between what I have or if I have time to figure something else out. Maybe eighteen will have to do."

"You've been working your ass off for how long now? Eighteen should be plenty."

She shook her head and went over to her easel area, looking between two pieces that I knew were nearly done. I didn't know how she could work on more than one thing at once. I could only work on one project at a time, but she put what was at the front of her mind out on the canvas, and if it happened to be something she had started on six months ago and needed a little more work, that's what she did.

Myra was a fantastic multi-tasker. It was a little scary.

"This whole project has been mostly portraits, although a little more abstract than usual. I've been harsher with my brush strokes recently, and I have a feeling it has more to do with the stress of my family than anything else. I'm not a fan of the way that's seeping into my work."

I looked at the two portraits, one of an older woman, someone I'd never met before in my life. She looked sad, at least until you saw her eyes. There, you saw a life long-lived, one filled with a past and perhaps hope for whatever future she held in her hands.

"This one's stunning. You can see every year she's lived."

"She is one of Dakota's regulars. I asked if I could sketch her for this project, and she readily agreed. She's always wanted to be in a painting, especially after the movie *Titanic* came out, and she kept joking with her late husband about him drawing her like one of his French girls."

I laughed and shook my head. "How many times have people actually used that line on you?"

"Mostly, it's been you," she said dryly and then laughed before I turned to see the other canvas.

I blinked, looking down at the man lying on his stomach on a soft bed, the angles of his back shown, a sheet covering enough for modesty but the rest on display.

His eyes were closed in sleep, a peaceful expression on his face. But there were scars, too, ones that would never go away, not after the accident.

"I didn't know you drew me," I said, my mouth going dry.

Myra twisted her fingers together. "This one's probably for me. Or you. I didn't ask. You were sleeping one day, and I got the urge to draw. And then I started painting, and here we are. You don't need to even look at this. I'm not going to show it to anyone."

I shook my head, then held my hand out as she tried to move the canvas away.

"I love it. I like that you covered my ass, so when my brothers see this, they won't make fun of me. But if you want to use it, go for it. Anything you want, Myra, you can have it."

She shook her head and pulled away again. Damn it, what was wrong?

"No, it's not right yet. Nothing is." She ran her hands through her hair, her motions jerky.

"What's wrong?"

She shook her head again. "Nothing. I'm just a little tired. And stressed out over this. And I guess my parents, too. I'm sorry. I'm always like this before a show, it just seems to be a little compounded right now. The painting's fine, but I don't think it's good enough for the exhibit."

I put my hand over my heart and took a staggering step back. "Ouch. I'm not good enough for your show?"

Her eyes widened, and I wanted to reach out and tell her that I was only kidding, but given the way she'd blanched, I felt like I had hit a nerve, and I didn't know how to make it better.

"Myra, I was only teasing you."

"No, you're right. This isn't right for the show. I don't even know what I'm doing here. I've done how many art shows now? Two or three like this at least. Why would anyone want to come and look at these paintings? They're not good enough. They're not like your friend on the other side of town."

"Lincoln has his style, and it's not in competition with yours. You get along with him."

"I know how well Lincoln does. He's brilliant. And I'm nowhere near his level."

"Is this nerves about the show? Or is this something else?"

She started to pace, wringing her hands together.

"I don't know. It's just a lot right now. Everything seems to be happening at once, and I think I need to breathe."

I froze, trying to catch up.

"Do you want to go for a drive? I haven't had a headache in a while. I'm good for driving you around.

We can go borrow Cross's Jeep and take the top down, drive to the mountains. Whatever you want."

She looked at me then, a mask on her face that I didn't recognize. "No, I don't need that. I don't know what I need, Nate. I need some time."

I swallowed hard, trying not to take her words as what they sounded like. A brush-off.

"You need time for the show? Or to go over what your parents are putting you through?"

"Maybe all of that? I don't know. I'm so afraid for the shoe to drop. Because you know my parents are going to try something. They want what my grandmother gave me. Sometimes, I feel like it would be easier if I just gave it to them."

I moved a step forward and took her hand. "We both know that's not the right answer. The law is on your side. Your parents will drop the suit."

She let out a laugh that didn't hold any humor. "We both know that's a lie. My parents are never going to stop until they get what they want. Look what they did to us. They made you believe I was some horrible person, and we both walked away because of it. They're going to do something more. I know it. They're going to try to hurt you or your family to get at me. And I don't know what I'm going to do about it."

I swallowed hard, trying to keep up.

"Everything is moving so fast. I haven't even had time to grieve, and now I have to deal with the stupidity that is this suit. They're contesting the will. They're saying that I did horrible things to get my grandmother to give me everything. And I didn't even want it. I only wanted her. I moved away from my parents and her because I couldn't stand being near the people who raised me. But I ended up putting distance between myself and the one person in my family I thought was really mine."

"She knew you loved her. And she loved you. She wrote about it in the will."

"And all it's doing is creating more rifts between my family and me. I'm just so tired, Nate. Between that and the show, it's a lot."

Something hovering beneath her words worried me, and I swallowed hard, afraid of what would happen if I turned over that stone.

"I'm here. You're not alone. All of us are here for you. Why don't we go back to the living room, get you some wine, and talk about it? Get everything out." Was I talking too fast? Could she hear the fear in my voice?

"Nate. I don't think it's going to be enough. Don't you see? Everything is happening so fast, and I can't keep up. And I'm so afraid that if I make the wrong choice, make another mistake, I'm going to lose everything and everyone. My parents have done so much, and it's hurt me. It breaks everybody in their path. I'm terrified if I take the wrong step, I'll turn into them and it'll hurt me, too."

I shook my head. "You are not them. You could never be."

"I ran when it got too hard before, and I lost you. I let myself believe that I could love again and now look at us."

I paused. "What are you talking about, Myra?"

"Look at us. We're right back where we started. Everything's moving so fast, and I can't keep up. I'm so afraid that I'm going to fuck up."

"Stop it. You're not going to fuck up. You are not fucking up."

"Nate. I messed up so badly before. I didn't... I just let myself fall into my parents' trap, and they're going to hurt you. They're going to find a way to hurt you, or your family, or our friends. And I don't know how to stop that from happening."

"You're not alone in this. Stop it, Myra. Can't you see that I'm not going anywhere? I fucking love you, Myra West."

We both froze, the words having ripped from me.

Her whole body went pale, her mouth dropping open. I felt like someone had punched me in the chest.

"Nate."

"No, don't say anything. Don't make it look as if I hit you when I told you I loved you."

"You loved me before. You don't know what you're thinking or feeling now. It's moving too fast."

I cursed and pulled away from her, pacing across her studio. "It hasn't been *that* fast. We've been in each other's lives for over a year now."

"We only learned the truth a few weeks ago. It's fast, Nate. We're not there. We can't be. If we go too fast again, we'll break like before. And I can't have that happen. I can't hurt you. Or lose everything because we're not thinking clearly enough."

I whirled on her, rage pounding within me even though I tried to push it back. "I get that you're scared, but you don't get to tell me how to feel."

"If you love me, that means you're going to be hurt even more when this breaks apart. You can't love me. We have to be friends. That's the only way we can't be hurt."

"That's a fucking lie. Because it hurts right now, Myra." That was an understatement. It felt as if she'd sliced me with her words, each one cutting and baring part of me I could never hide again.

And the thing was…I knew she was only doing it to hurt herself. This wasn't about me. This was about her and her pain. Unfortunately, I couldn't see a way through it.

"Why is this so hard for you?" I said again. "Why can't you think through what your parents are doing to you? They're not pulling us apart right now. *You're* doing it."

"I'm not ready, Nate. I can't be on your timetable. I need to think things through and try to make sure that nobody gets hurt in the end. Because I don't know what I'd do if I lost you."

"What do you think love is? It's that big breath you take when you're finally able to trust that someone will always be there for you."

"But nobody's ever been there for me before," she shouted back. "How am I supposed to believe in that now? Why can't we just take some more time to be sure? I need to be sure."

"You're not making any fucking sense."

"We thought we loved each other before, Nate. But we didn't trust each other enough to believe in that. I don't want to make that mistake again. If we cut ties and not let our relationship move forward now, then we can still be in each other's lives. No one has to get broken from this."

"Are you even hearing yourself? You don't even make any sense."

"I have to make sense. I care about you, Nate. I don't want to lose the family that we've made. But if my parents do something or figure out what your feelings truly are, it'll be harder to walk away later."

"Seriously, are you listening to yourself?"

"Stop pushing me. I can't be on your timetable."

"Then I need to go. Because I fucking love you, and apparently, you don't love me."

"Nate."

"No. Once you figure out what the fuck you're thinking, I might be around. But you're wrong. If we decide to leave each other now or later, it's going to hurt no matter what. There's no hiding from that."

"Then why were we even together in the first place?"

"I'm starting to question that, too."

She covered her face with her hands, her whole body shaking. "We fell into this, and it's moved quickly. Why can't we simply take some time to breathe and figure out exactly what we're feeling without all of the mess of hormones, need, and lust?"

"Because feelings don't work like that, Myra. You can't all be icy and cold and practical when it comes to emotions."

She took a step back as if I'd hit her, and I cursed under my breath. "Myra…"

"No, you should go. Because we're doing what I knew we would. We're lashing out, and hurting each other. And I want to like you in the end, Nathan. You should go. So I can still like you."

"Myra. I love you."

"And I don't want to lose you."

"Then why are we already lost?" I asked and then turned on my heel and left.

Chapter 19

Myra

The idea that I could make a mistake so severe in such a short period of time shouldn't surprise me. I had done it before, after all. And yet, all I wanted to do was curl up into a ball and pretend that I hadn't pushed away the man I thought I loved. I was so stressed out and worried about what might come that I forgot to look at what was right in front of me. I needed to fix that.

Nate had left the night before, and I had sat in my studio on my little couch, crying until I had nothing left in me. The girls had texted, but I didn't think they knew anything. Nate wouldn't have told his brothers—wouldn't have told anyone. He would have hidden himself away in his house and cuddled Daisy as he tried to deal with his emotions. The idea that I knew so much about him and yet couldn't trust his feelings or my own shamed me.

I had made a mistake, and I needed to stand up and say that I was sorry. I needed to tell him that I cared for him. Did I love him? That was the problem. I thought I did, and yet it was all tangled up in everything I had felt for him before, and all of that dissolved into a churning emotion that I couldn't quite name.

I didn't want to tell him that I loved him only to realize I didn't. That wouldn't be fair to either of us.

But it was cruel for me to throw his love back at him and tell him that he was wrong as I pretended that we could find our way out of the ashes and embers whole.

I should have told him that I needed more time, but I still wanted to be with him. Instead, I'd gotten scared and pushed him away completely. That was what the cold and calculating Myra did. But the warm Myra who had married Nate hadn't been silly and stupid like that. She had believed in what she felt.

I needed to trust that person again.

I trusted Nate. I didn't trust myself, however.

I had to make sure he understood that. And so, I

would go to him. I would tell him I was sorry about what happened last night and say that I wanted more time. That I never wanted to hurt him.

I hoped like hell he would forgive me.

My phone rang, and I frowned and looked down at the readout.

It was my lawyer. Dread pooled in my belly.

"Hello?" I asked.

"Hello, Ms. West?"

"You can call me Myra." We had been talking practically daily at this point.

He let out a rough chuckle. He didn't sound too worried. I had to hope that was a good thing. "I wanted to let you know that the case isn't going through."

I frowned, trying to understand what he was saying. "My family dropped the case?" I asked, trying not to hope.

"It seems their lawyer doesn't want to pursue it. I don't know all of the circumstances, and I'm going to get them to you as soon as I do know, but they're not filing any claims. I have a feeling that when they talked to whoever finally looked at what they were dealing with, they decided it would be a lost cause."

Relief filled me, but I didn't want to believe it. "Are you sure?" I asked, a coppery taste on my tongue. It was stress, I knew that, but I felt like I might throw up.

"They can still file to contest the will through another lawyer, but their current attorney has dropped the case. That means, for now, we're going forward with everything. We're doing everything by the book, but you and Lacey, as well as the others in the will, should be fine."

"What? I can't believe their lawyer would tell them to drop it."

"He was also your grandmother's lawyer in California. She may have had someone here to handle the will, but he worked closely with her in California. He likely knew everything, and because he couldn't tell his clients, your parents are now realizing they don't have a leg to stand on. They may try for something later, but for now, you're free and clear. I know we have a lot to discuss with the estate and the charities and other things on the docket, and we'll get there eventually. But you're not alone in this, Myra. I just wanted to let you know."

I said a few words, thanking him and saying I would be in touch soon. And then, I tried to catch my breath.

I wasn't alone.

He'd said the words, and they were true.

Oh, my parents would keep trying to take what Grandma Sharon left. They would do something. And they would never go away, even if I cut all ties to them.

But this was one small victory, a bit of the weight off my shoulders.

I felt like I could breathe again, and it reminded me how much of an idiot I was when it came to Nate.

I needed to tell him about this. I needed to tell him so much.

I looked down at my phone, considered texting him to say I was on my way over, but I didn't want him to push me away. Instead, I pulled out my purse and tucked my feet into my shoes. I would meet him at his house and find a way to grovel. He had been the one to grovel before. Now, it was my turn.

I only hoped he didn't hate me. I couldn't go back to the feelings we'd had before. The animosity between us. It wouldn't be good for either of us—or the family we had made.

The doorbell rang, and my heart flew into my throat. Was it Nate? I hoped to hell it was.

I practically ran to the front door and pulled it open with a flourish, but it wasn't him.

"Roland?"

"Hey, cuz. We need to talk." He pushed his way into my living room, knocking me back slightly as he did. I staggered. He closed the door behind him and locked it, and fear crawled up my spine.

"Roland, you need to go. I did not say you could enter my home."

"*Your* home. *Your* will. Everything is all *yours*. Just like it's always been. Miss perfect Myra. She gets everything she wants. I'm not surprised that this went in your favor. You probably blew the judge and the lawyers and everybody else to get what you wanted. You've always been good on your knees."

I grimaced, shaking my head. "I don't know where you're getting this, but you need to go. I know you're angry, but this has nothing to do with me."

He moved forward so quickly I almost missed it. His arm lashed out, and he hit my cheek hard. I moved back, falling to the floor. My phone fell out of my hands, skidding across the hardwood. I reached up and cupped my face, the sting shocking, the skin warm.

"Did you…hit me?" I asked, gasping.

"Shut up. Just shut the fuck up. How dare you? How *dare* you leave this family and think you can have everything. I don't know what you said to our dear old grandmother, but you are not taking this from me. I need that money. And now, I have nothing. All because you are a fucking whore."

He lashed out again, but this time, I covered my face, blocking him.

"Stop it. Go away."

I moved to get my phone, but he shoved me. I fell to my knees, the wood sending pinpricks of pain through my body. My wrist turned, and I fell, screaming out in pain as my shoulder hit the floor.

I scrambled up, ignoring the pain in my shoulder and wrist and knee. "What is wrong with you?"

"You've taken everything from me. I need that money. Without it, I'm broke. I tried to make you understand before, but you didn't listen. I even thought if I could get you out of the way when I ran that stop sign, it would help, but it didn't. Then, when I saw you at the concert? I figured I'd find a way to make you see reason. How the hell am I supposed to survive on nothing? You took everything, and now you're going to pay."

There was madness in his eyes, a darkness that was unlike anything I had ever seen before. He'd tried to hurt me? All those times I'd thought I'd only been seeing things, but he'd been right there. Waiting. Watching. Trying to hurt me.

I struggled to get up again, then pushed at him, kicking at him with my high heel. He groaned, slapping at me, but I was faster than he was this time. He blocked the front door, but I could still go out the back. I ran, looking for my phone but unable to reach it. I had a landline back there if I could get to it. I needed to get away from Roland. Call the authorities. Do something.

He was twice my size, and so much stronger. I wasn't able to fight back effectively, but I could run.

And so, I did, my heels slamming against the wood and then the tile as I made my way to the other side of the house.

But Roland was faster. He tugged at my hair, and I screamed. I fell back, my head slamming against the tile as he pushed and shoved.

My mouth went dry, and I closed my eyes, the world spinning. I tried to get up, but then he was there, and I saw a flash of something bright in front of my eyes. Suddenly, a searing pain shocked my system.

Warmth spread over my flesh, and I looked down at my forearm, feeling as if I were watching a movie instead of living this. I quickly clamped my hand over the bleeding wound. Roland had cut me with the butcher knife from my kitchen, a long line running from my elbow to my wrist, and it was deep enough that I was afraid I could see bone.

I gagged, bile filling my throat as the pain set in, and shock slammed into me.

"Look at what you made me do. I didn't mean to do that, Myra. But you were so fast. I only wanted to threaten you. Jesus Christ, Myra. *Look what you made me do.*"

I was shaking, my back against the wall as I scooted away from him, trying to stop the bleeding. But it wouldn't stop. It kept coming. I didn't think he had nicked an artery because it wasn't spurting, but it was bad. Fucking bad. Blood seeped out from between my fingers, and the pressure I applied wasn't enough. Roland threw a towel at my face. I took it like a lifeline and pressed it to the wound, trying to wrap it around my arm.

"You need to stop the bleeding and be okay. You need to be able to sign over the money to me."

I looked at him as he ran his hands over his face, the knife still clutched in his hand, the blade pointed outwards. My blood coated it.

I looked down at my wound and then turned to the side and threw up what little I'd had that morning for breakfast.

"You're disgusting. What the hell, Myra? *Why did you make me do this*?"

I couldn't wipe my face, but I tried to push the pain from my mind and focus. I needed to remain calm. It was the only way I could survive. "Please, call an ambulance. We'll tell them it was an accident. I swear I will say everything was an accident and you didn't mean to cut me. But I need to go to the hospital. Please, Roland. You didn't mean to do this."

"This is all your fault. They're going to blame me, but it's all your fault."

"You're right, it is my fault," I lied, my vision going

blurry. “It’s all my fault. All you need to do is call them and tell them it’s my fault. I will agree. I’ll be the one who goes to jail and everything. I just need you to call the hospital.”

I was losing too much blood, and I could barely breathe.

Roland looked at me and nodded tightly. “Yes, that’s what we’ll tell them. And you’ll give me the money?”

“Of course, I’ll give you the money. I’ll give you anything. Please, call an ambulance.”

“Myra?”

I froze as I looked into Roland’s eyes. Suddenly, the world went quiet.

Nate had come into the studio, maybe thinking I would still be there. I had forgotten that door, everything coming at me so quickly.

Roland’s back was to Nate, but as he turned, Nate’s eyes went wide, and Roland slashed.

“Myra,” Nate shouted and then grunted as he leaned forward, holding his hand over a cut in his side.

“No!” I said and tried to scramble up. I crawled over to them and pushed myself toward Roland’s legs. Roland and Nate fought each other, both of them trying to go for the knife, but I moved more strategically, using what little strength I had, and took Roland out at the knees. Nate pushed, and then there was screaming, a sound that would echo in my dreams for however many moments I had left. And then Roland stopped making any noise at all. I looked down at the blade buried partway into Roland's chest and then at Nate, who was on his knees in front of me.

"Myra. Myra, don't go."

"Nate."

I looked at him, tried to reach for him, but my arms weren't moving.

Nate was saying something, doing something with his phone, maybe. I didn't know.

I tried to tell him that I loved him. That I was sorry. But no words came out.

Instead, I closed my eyes, and I rested on Nate's chest.

And warmth slid over me.

Chapter 20

Nate

"It's getting damn exhausting coming back to this place," Cross said as he looked around the small hospital room.

I nodded, leaning back and trying not to move my side too much. "I have to tell you, I don't really like being back in this bed. It might've been a few years, but I'm over getting stitches."

Cross winced. "Is it bad that I didn't even think about your accident when I mentioned that?"

I shook my head and then winced. I was grateful for the pain meds they had given me. I had a headache from hell thanks to the stress and adrenaline of seeing Myra on the floor like that. And, of course, from the slice to my side. I needed a little bit of rest—and to see Myra.

"No, I get you. I was thinking about the fact that every single one of us has been in the hospital for something or other recently. All of it added up is a bit much."

"I'm just glad you're okay." He paused. "And Myra's going to be fine."

I opened my eyes to look at my brother, my throat going dry. "She's really going to be okay? It's not only the doctors telling Paris, and therefore Paris telling you random things to placate me?"

"Paris is on Myra's emergency contact list. The doctors told her everything. She's out of surgery now, and she's going to be fine. She'll probably have to go through some rehab and physical therapy for her arm, but they don't think she's going to lose any range of motion or sensation."

"It was her left arm, at least. Not the one she paints with," I said softly.

"Jesus. I didn't even think about that. You and I aren't firing on all cylinders tonight."

"A knife wound or two will do that to you." I paused. "She's not going to wake up alone, is she? She feels alone enough as it is. She can't wake up alone."

"One of the girls will be there. You don't need to worry about that."

"We both know that's all I'm going to do."

"I know. That's what we do. I'm pretty sure we're going to have to get a hospital wing here, though, because this is exhausting."

"I'm sorry we got stabbed. I know it must be hard on you," I said, only a little bite in my tone.

"Take it out on me. The more you do, the easier it'll be when you get out of here and don't have all this rage inside you."

"You weren't that bad after the shooting."

Cross frowned. "I talked to people. And I had Hazel."

"Macon was the one who didn't have anyone."

Cross shook his head. "No, he didn't. He could have had us, but he closed himself off. And he didn't have Dakota until it was almost too late. So, he fought, and bloodied himself, and he got out his rage that way. You're probably going to be angry for a long time."

"The cut on my side wasn't that deep."

Cross narrowed his eyes. "Fourteen stitches, Nate. It was deep enough."

"No, it was just long. And it bled a lot. Myra, though? That cut was horrendous."

"I didn't get a look at it, and I'm kind of glad I didn't."

"I was an EMT for long enough, Cross. I saw some shitty things. That was one of the worst."

My brother studied my face. "It could be that it was the worst because it was on a woman you love."

My heart ached at that, and I shook my head. "She doesn't love me, Cross."

"That's bullshit."

"She told me she cared for me and then pushed me out of the house once I told her I loved her. Pretty sure that seals the deal."

Cross looked at me and shook his head. "She's scared. You have both been through a lot. And that was *before* her cousin decided to go fucking insane. But she loves you. It might take her some time to realize that. And you should give it to her. Don't rush into that. It's how you make mistakes."

I closed my eyes and groaned. "Yeah, I made horrible mistakes before when it came to Myra, I guess it's routine for us."

"Don't let it be. She's going to get out of the hospital soon, just like you, and you guys will fix this."

"I don't know if we can."

A pause. "Do you want to?"

I looked up at my brother and swallowed hard. "I do. I love her. And she's so strong, Cross. She crawled on the floor, bruised and bleeding out to help me. I thought I was strong enough to push Roland down and away, but that guy was muscular. He was big and knew how to fight."

"He's not going to bother you again."

"Am I supposed to feel something that he's dead? I don't feel anything. Does that make me a psychopath?" I asked, only partly joking.

Cross gave me a look. "Once you're off the pain meds and not in shock, you'll feel something. And it's going to be horrible. And you'll wonder if you're ever going to get over it. But you'll talk to people. You're going to talk with Arden and me. You know we've been through this before."

I let out a rough laugh and then reached up to wipe the tears from my face. "How did our family end up like this? How is this even happening?"

"I just hope this is the end. That, after this, you and Myra find each other, and we never have to be in this hospital except for good things." He paused. "By the way, Mom and Dad are on their way."

I let out a soft laugh. "I'm surprised it took you that long to mention that."

"They were on the first plane out. And, Nate? They're moving back."

I blinked. "I thought Mom and Dad loved it there."

"They do, but you know Dad's retiring, and he wants to settle here."

"Because of us?"

"Of course, because of us. Mom and Dad had a great opportunity over there, and it was good for them."

I nodded. "I never held that against them. It was the best thing for the two of them."

"Now, they don't want to miss out on anything."

"I don't plan on being in the hospital again."

Cross shrugged. "I hope to hell not. But that's not the only reason they're coming here. Liam and Arden are adopting. There's going to be a few weddings coming up. And grandbabies."

"You and Hazel?" I asked.

"Yep, she wants kids. And hell, so do I. And I know Dakota and Macon are already talking about adding a brother or sister to their family for Joshua so the age gap isn't too big. And, hello, Joshua is their grandkid now. Of course, Mom and Dad want to be around."

"I'm kind of afraid of what kind of child Prior and Paris will create," I laughed.

"I'm going to have to agree with you. But if we ever say that in front of her, Paris will create a voodoo doll of each of us. We know this."

I laughed and then groaned, holding my side. "Okay, no more laughing," I said, trying not to laugh again.

"Deal." Cross sobered. "I'm so sorry you got hurt."

"It's par for the course with us."

"So let's make sure it never happens again. This sucked. All of us getting hurt as much as we have. Let's not let it happen again."

"I'll try. But, Jesus, I'm never going to get the sight of Myra out of my mind. She lost so much blood, Cross."

"And she survived. You got there in time." My brother paused. "How did you know to be there?"

I shook my head and regretted the movement again. "I was there to apologize and to try to fix the shit we were going through. There was a car in the driveway, and no one answered the doorbell, so I went around the side of the house and hoped the studio door was unlocked."

"Good timing," Cross muttered.

"I heard her talking, even though it was mumbled. I think she was trying to convince him to call the ambulance."

"Maybe he would have, but we don't know for sure. Regardless, you saved her."

"She saved me."

"So, what are you going to do?" Cross asked after a moment, and I swallowed hard.

"She needs time to heal. And the girls need to be with her."

"You're not going to back out, are you?" Cross's voice went stony.

"No. I'll go to her. But she needs to heal," I repeated.

"So do you. You can do that together."

"She was so scared, Cross. I don't want to hurt her any more."

Cross gave me a look as if he understood, but I wasn't sure I did.

Instead, I closed my eyes and tried to rest. I knew that no matter what happened the next time I saw her, I would never be able to get the sight of her bleeding out on the floor, unconscious in my arms, out of my mind.

It would haunt my nightmares until the end of time.

And I wasn't sure how I was supposed to deal with that.

Chapter 21

Myra

I LEANED AGAINST MY PILLOWS AND WANTED TO crawl into a hole and sleep forever. That probably wasn't the best thing to think, but everything hurt. I wanted to go home, feel better, and find a way to work through everything going through my mind.

Paris had finally left, and I had a moment to myself, even though I knew the nurses would likely walk in at any moment.

I wanted to see Nate. And yet, I didn't want to see him. I was so afraid of what I should say to him, and it worried me. I'd fought for my life, but I'd gotten hurt in the process.

I likely wouldn't be here right now if it weren't for him, but he wouldn't be in the hospital a few doors down from me if it weren't for me. I needed to find him and tell him that I loved him. To say I was sorry. But I didn't know when the right time for that was.

The door opened, and I looked up, expecting a nurse. Instead, dread filled my belly. My father walked in, then closed the door firmly behind him as he looked at me. I'd never quite seen that expression on my father's face before. He was pale, and there was fear in his gaze. And yet, I could barely see it.

He had never looked at me like this before. As if I were worth more than simply what I could do for him.

"Myra," he said, his voice rough.

"I'm surprised they let you in," I said, my voice icy.

He nodded, his face going slack a bit. "I deserve that. But I am your father. We share the same last name. They let me through because I'm family."

"I guess that makes sense."

"I can go if you want me to, but I came to check on you."

"As you can see, I'm okay." I didn't move my arm, it hurt too much to do so, but his gaze focused on it anyway, and then on the bruise on my face, and the one on my chin.

He shook his head. "You're not okay, Myra."

"I will be."

"I didn't know Roland was going to act like that," my father said suddenly, and I looked at him and nodded.

"I believe you. I don't think anybody realized that Roland was capable of what he did." I tried not to hear his scream again, the last sound my cousin made before he died. But it was there, scratching at me, clawing at my spine, tearing up my body and my soul.

"I don't know if it's something we did or if he just cracked, but I wanted to say I'm sorry."

I looked up at my father, stunned. "Why are you apologizing?"

"Because your mother and I made selfish choices to try and get more. We always made selfish choices when it came to you. And I can't figure out why. It seems to be what we do these days. And we hurt you in the process. Somehow, Roland took after us and came after you. I didn't know that he'd spent all his money. I didn't know any of that. I feel like I failed you."

I couldn't quite believe this, and I didn't know if I trusted his words. Maybe he was trying to absolve his soul and explain his choices, but they weren't mine.

"I don't blame you for what Roland did, or for the decisions he made, but I don't know how I can forgive you for everything else."

He looked at me and nodded, swallowing hard. "I don't deserve your forgiveness. I don't even know why I'm saying the things I am right now. Maybe Roland's mental break changed something in me."

While I wanted to believe that my father was genuinely remorseful for the snide comments he'd made, for breaking up Nate and me, and pushing me out of the family, I didn't think he was truly remorseful. He would have to acknowledge them first.

I did believe that he felt bad that I had gotten hurt. Because I knew that even though my parents had lashed out and cut me emotionally my entire life, they had never once laid a hand on me in anger or hatred. It was something I truly believed my father never would have done.

"I'm tired. Thank you for coming."

"Thank you for letting me be here and not kicking me out right away."

I paused. "I thought about it."

My father nodded. "I don't blame you."

"I don't know if I can ever forgive you for everything you did. I don't know if I want to. But I do know that you had nothing to do with Roland."

My father nodded, his jaw tightening.

"And I don't blame you for any of that. But I am tired. You should go."

"I'm sorry. I'll fix this. I'll find a way."

I held back a laugh as it would only cause me pain. "Mom's not even here with you. A single conversation while I'm drugged up and in pain isn't going to fix anything. I left the family long ago, Dad. And I don't know if I ever want to come back, especially now. I don't know if I'll ever be able to forgive you for what you did—for what you've always done to me. But I do know that I'll never forget it. And it's not about the money, it's what you did to Nate and me. What you've done to me my entire life. You need to go. If I decide that I want to make another connection, I will contact you. Until then, you need to think long and hard about why you are here trying to apologize for something you don't even truly understand yet. Someone doesn't change in a blink of an eye. So, thank you for being here, but you need to go now."

I was exhausted, out of energy, and I didn't want to speak anymore. My father gave me a nod, met my gaze, and then walked out. As he did though, he froze, and it wasn't until he moved out of the way that I realized why.

"Nate," I whispered.

The love of my life looked at me, leaning against the wall in scrub pants and a hospital gown.

"I found you," he whispered.

And I promptly burst into tears.

Chapter 22

Nate

Alarmed, I cursed and staggered my way to the chair next to her. I fell into it, winced at the pain in my side, and reached to grab her hand.

"Don't cry, baby. I can go." I let out a breath in a hiss. "After I catch my breath. I'm not actually supposed to be here right now."

"Why *are* you here? You should be hooked up to an IV or something. You were bleeding, Nate."

I looked down at her arm, and bile rose to my throat. "You were the one bleeding, Myra. Oh, God, I thought I'd lost you."

I reached over, careful of my stitches, thankful for the pain meds running through my body, and cupped her face. "You're bruised."

"I'll heal."

"So will I. But I'm never going to forget the sight of you on that floor."

"Same here. I don't know what I would have done if you hadn't walked through that door. I was trying to get Roland to call an ambulance, and I thought maybe he would, but he probably would have run. And I don't think I would have had enough energy to call anyone."

Tears fell down both of our faces then, and I leaned forward and brushed hers away. "I was there. We both were. You saved me, too, baby."

"I think I sort of just fell into him. You would have had it."

I let out a shaky breath. "We saved each other, how's that?"

"I'd rather not have had any of that happen."

That made me smile. God, I loved this woman. "Okay, I'll take that, too."

I wanted to hold her, but neither of us was in any shape to do that. Instead, I simply gripped her right hand and leaned against the bed as we stared at each other, both of us exhausted and too tired to even speak. A nurse would probably come in at any moment and pull me away, so I had to talk quickly.

"I love you," I whispered. Her eyes widened, and I squeezed her right hand. "You can tell me to go away again. You can say you need more time, and I will understand that. But I want you to know that I love you. And if it's too fast for you, then we'll deal with that. Take it one step at a time. But like before, I shouldn't have run away. I shouldn't have left you alone. I'm never going to run again. I'll go if you tell me to, but I won't run. I will always be here if you need me. I want you in my life, Myra. Any way I can get you. I almost lost you yesterday. I almost lost the best thing in my life, the person who brings me hope, and beauty, and everything I need. And I never want that to happen."

Tears fell again, and I brushed them away once more.

"I can't believe I almost lost you," she choked out, and I swallowed hard. "I was on my way to you, by the way. To tell you that I didn't want you to leave. That I wanted to stay and work things out and find a way to make us work."

Relief flooded me. "We can do that—you and me. We'll go as slowly as you want. We probably should have started glacier-slow to begin with. But it's hard for me when you're around. You burn everything up inside me. You bring me to life."

"And you saved mine," she whispered. "When I

was fading, I tried to say the words, but I couldn't. I didn't have enough energy."

I frowned, looking down at her even though she was so exhausted. "What words?" I whispered.

"I love you, too. I always have. I love you, Nathan. Don't go. Don't run. And don't let me run. Let's just be."

I leaned forward and kissed her softly. When I moved back, she was asleep, the pain clearly too much. I did my best to lean against her bed, trying not to hurt my stitches or her, and let my eyes close. The nurse would eventually come for me, and I would get yelled at, but it didn't matter.

I had almost lost the woman I loved, the one I had fallen for the moment I ran into her that day on the quad when we were late for coffee. I had fallen in love with her when she stole my food, and I had done the same to her. When she let me kiss her for the first time and then be with her after. I loved her when she yelled at me, and when pain crossed her face for the stupidity I brought to her life. She was the only person outside of my family who had always been steady in my life, even if it was only a memory at times.

She was my first, my only, and now, she would be my forever.

And though I had nearly lost her again to make

this happen, I hadn't. And I would never let her go again. I knew she would never let me go either.

I had found my first. And my only.

I had found my promise.

Epilogue

Myra

"I THINK WE'RE LIVING IN A ZOO. OR MAYBE A CIRCUS," Nate said, leaning against the back of the couch. I snuggled into him, and he kissed the top of my head.

"Perhaps. But I think I like all the noise. Who knew?"

Macon's two dogs chased after Arden's Jasper and our Daisy with Joshua following behind, laughing and trying to make barking sounds. Macon shook his head, then went after them as if he were going to wrangle the crew.

Dakota looked over from the kitchen island where she set up dinner, laughing at the two loves of her life before going back to work.

Paris was trying to help, but kept getting her hand slapped for daring to touch Dakota's deviled eggs with her special new recipe.

Dakota let out an exasperated breath. "Seriously. It's fine. It does not have to be at the perfect angle."

"It's like you don't even know me," Paris complained.

"Come on, darling. It is time to go sit over with Nate and Myra and see how they're doing."

Paris scowled. "You only want me out of the kitchen so Dakota cooks faster."

"I can't help it if you're right," Nate added on a laugh.

I held back a laugh at Prior and looked over as Paris stomped her way over to where we sat and took a seat herself.

"I feel like I'm never appreciated." Paris mock-pouted.

"I appreciate you," I said, leaning into Nate.

"You're only saying that because you're cuddling with the love of your life and acting all lovey-dovey. Believe me, it doesn't last," she growled, and Nate blew her air-kisses.

"I'm kidding," Paris added quickly." I shouldn't even joke like that," she muttered.

"Good, because I was going to have to hurt you," Prior said as he moved into the living room, kissing the top of Paris's head as he winked at me.

"You two feeling okay?" Hazel asked as she joined us.

I let out a sigh, the same as Nate. "Yes, for the eighteenth time, we're both fine. We could stand, you know. Help out."

"If you two stand up, we will push you right back down," Cross growled. "Don't make me hurt you."

"He sure is grumbly," I muttered, and Nate snorted.

"Oh, this is him in a good mood. You should have seen him before he met Hazel."

"Hey," Cross said.

"Nate's not wrong," Arden added, coming into the room with Liam following behind her. "Okay, I am going to go help Dakota because now that Paris has been kicked out of the kitchen, she's all on her own."

"No, no, we have it." Nate's mother waved her hands, his father right by her.

"Yes. All of you guys just take a seat and let me help my future daughter-in-law," Nate's mother said, clapping her hands before making her way into the kitchen. Because the room was large and open-concept, everybody was pretty much hanging out in the same area anyway. Still, I knew Dakota liked having a little bit of space. However, one look at the three of them together, and I knew that this was what Dakota wanted. She wanted to get to know her future in-laws, two people I was now getting to know, as well.

It was weird to think that I was only just now finding out who they were and how we fit together. Even though I had once been married to their son, this was all new.

That hadn't been an easy conversation at all, telling them about our marriage and divorce, but there was no going back. We had made our apologies, and now we were living with our consequences. But nobody held a grudge. I think we were all simply happy to be alive and able to annoy and be annoyed by each other.

"Okay, dinner's ready. We're sitting around the house, not at the table since I don't think we have one big enough for all of us," Dakota commented, looking around her. "Macon, you're going to have to convince your brother to build something."

"I already had it on the list," Cross said. "I'll build a big enough table, but I'm trying to figure out whose house can handle it." Cross narrowed his eyes and studied all of us before his gaze rested on mine. "Myra, you do have the largest dining room."

Liam frowned. "Really? Even me?" Liam questioned.

"We know, we know, everything you have is big, darling," Arden soothed, and everyone in the room groaned.

"Never say that again," Nate said, visibly shuddering next to me.

"What? I'm just telling the truth," Arden singsonged.

I couldn't hold back my laughter. I loved Nate's twin, and I was so happy that she was going to be my sister again.

I looked down at the shiny ring on my finger and smiled. I had pulled it out of my jewelry box when I came home from the hospital, and Nate had been right beside me as I did, looking down at the ring that he had once worn. We both looked at each other, and without words, had slid the rings onto our fingers. There was no need to propose, to ask each other to be with one another for the rest of our days. We would have that, and we would take the next step when it was time.

We were a family now, and as I looked at the people around me, I smiled.

"I would welcome a large table in my dining room. The one that I have now might fit everyone, but as the families grow, I might need a larger one."

"I'll fit one to your style perfectly," Cross said. He looked over at Liam. "And I'll make one for you, too. That way, we don't always bug Myra and Nate."

"I take it I'm moving into your place," Nate said, giving me a look.

I blushed and shrugged. "I need my studio. Plus, where's the table going to go?"

Nate snorted and then kissed me softly. "Okay, sounds like a plan." He kissed my ring finger, and everybody oohed and aahed, even Joshua, who came back, puppies immediately piled on top of him.

Cross sighed. "Looks like I'll be busy for a while."

"I don't mind. It just means we're going to be together for a long time," Hazel said. "I mean, the pact is over, I guess. Everybody got their blind dates."

I looked around at the others. The girls grinned. "Even if it didn't come about the way we planned."

"Hey, I'm everything you planned," Nate complained.

"Of course, of course, my love. What was I thinking?" I rolled my eyes, and everybody laughed.

"Be nice, he still has stitches," Paris admonished.

"See? Even Paris says you need to be nice to me." Nate paused. "If she agrees, maybe you don't need to be nice."

Paris narrowed her eyes. "Hey, Prior, hit him for me, will you?"

"Nobody is going to be hitting anybody. Behave, children," Mrs. Brady said, winking at me.

"I'm so glad we're moving back," Mr. Brady added. "That means I get to know the new ladies in my boys' lives, and Liam, and this little one over here."

Joshua beamed at his new grandpa. "And all the puppies. And kittens. We have a lot of cats."

Macon rolled his eyes, and their father grinned. "So I hear. I can't wait to get to know all of them. You guys have created a pretty spectacular family here. Thank you for letting us join."

I wiped away tears as the other girls sniffed. Nate looked at me and shook his head.

He leaned down. "Dad is good with the speeches. He's like Captain America in that way."

I laughed like he wanted me to, and then leaned into the man I loved.

The pact sisters and the Brady brothers, as well as Arden and Liam, had found their way to each other, even if it wasn't in the most conventional of ways—or easy.

But as I held up my glass and cheered and toasted the three women I had made a promise to, I knew that no matter what past we each came from, the future would always be paved with family and hope and greater promises.

And, of course, a very special Brady.

Next up from Carrie Ann is MY ONE NIGHT! Dillon and Elise are ready for their romance!

Want to read a special BONUS EPILOGUE featuring Nate & Myra? CLICK HERE!

Bonus Epilogue

Nate

"Looks like you're going to do this right," Cross remarked as he leaned over and helped me with my tie.

"My tie is fine. You didn't need to help," I grumbled.

"Apparently, when Nate is stressed out, he lashes out. Who knew?" Prior said, and I flipped him off.

"That's the love we need in this room. It's your wedding day, so you should growl and flip off everybody." Macon rolled his eyes, and I let out a breath.

"This is my second wedding to Myra. Why am I so stressed out?"

"Probably because the first one you had with her included an Elvis impersonator?" Cross asked.

"It was not an Elvis impersonator. It was a Dolly Parton impersonator. I don't know why you can't get that right." I laughed as he looked at me, dumbfounded, and I shook my head. "I hope that I do this right this time. That I don't fuck up."

Cross glared. "Of course, you're not going to fuck it up. You've learned from your mistakes, and since you're the final Brady to get married, you have now seen how to get it done right."

"I know, always in last place," Prior joked, shaking his head.

"Forever the bridesmaid, but at least now, you're the bride," Macon added drily.

"I don't feel the love with you guys. Was I this bad for your weddings?"

"Yes," they all answered at once, and we all broke out laughing.

"Why do I have to wear a tie?" Joshua said, tugging at his. "It's not fair," the little guy said as he came into the room, Dakota behind him.

She had on a champagne-colored dress that hugged her curves, and I knew it was different than the other girls'. Each one had picked the same color but a dress that fit their style, and from the way Macon's eyes glazed over, he liked her style a lot.

"You have to wear a suit today, like you did the other days. I'm sorry you've been so blessed with being a ring bearer four times now, but you're just going to have to get over yourself."

"But I was at least the best man before," Joshua griped, and then his eyes brightened. "Ooh, cheese and crackers."

"Not while you're in that suit," Dakota scolded, a smile on her face.

"I've got him. You go take care of the bride," Macon said, kissing Dakota softly. "He'll be fine."

"I've got him, too," Prior said, holding Joshua back as the kid comically tried to reach for the cheese and crackers.

"And, he's right, he was my best man. That means our wedding was the best," Macon added, winking at me.

"Stop it," Dakota said as I laughed. "No more playing who's the best at weddings. Because we all know that Paris would win."

"Hell yeah," Prior cheered, and I blinked at Dakota.

"You didn't even pick your wedding?" I shook my head.

She shrugged. "Of course, not. If I did, then Paris would drone on and on. So we're just not going to do that. She wins. Prior doesn't because he cheered like a lunatic. But, no, we're going to let Paris take this one. Since it's your wedding today, we can pretend it's all about you and Myra. But it's pretty much always about Paris."

"It's the hormones, isn't it?" I winced.

"Do not say that to her," Prior whispered, his eyes wide, and not a lick of humor on his face. "If you make a pregnancy and hormone joke to her, she *will* hurt you."

"Wow, you seem scared," I said with a laugh, but no one else joined in.

"Pregnancy hormones are no joke," Prior said, letting out a breath. "We're just going to get through this wedding. And whatever Paris wants, she gets."

"You have, like, a few more months of this, don't you?" Cross asked softly.

"You're dealing with it with Hazel. You understand."

"My hormones weren't that bad with Joshua." Dakota put her hand on her flat belly. "Let's hope they're not bad with this one." She grinned as Macon kissed her again, and I shooed them out.

"Okay, we need to get ready. We don't want to be late."

"Like Paris would let this thing run late," Dakota said, laughing.

"How did you get them all pregnant at the same time?" I asked, shaking my head.

"Yes, how *did* that happen?" Joshua asked, and Macon flipped me off over the kid's head.

"It was magic. You know, fairy magic."

Joshua gave Cross a weird look. "Okay. I guess. Are we ready to go?"

I looked at my brothers and my nephew and nodded. "Yes. let's go meet my ex-wife, who's now going to be my new wife."

"How many times have you said that, and she's hit you?" Macon asked drily.

"Enough that I'm forming a callus over the spot." I grinned.

We made our way out to the ceremony area, and I looked up at Arden, who stood under the archway. My twin and best friend smiled at me, her dress gorgeous, and her hair done in long waves. She waved.

"I'm so honored that you asked me to officiate." Arden kissed my cheek. "It only makes sense that your twin should be the one to do it."

"I'm kind of sad that we didn't think about doing it for your wedding."

"No, I'm pretty sure if we hadn't had the minister

do it, we would have had a Montgomery. You know there's like, a hundred of them around."

"I heard that," Liam said from his chair, surrounded by, of course, a few dozen Montgomerys.

"Let's get this show on the road," I said, rubbing my hands together.

My brothers stood at my side, and as the music began, memories of the first time I had seen Myra played through my mind—the first time I'd kissed her, the first time we'd made love. Memories of every moment we had together cascaded through my memories in an instant. But when the music changed, and Myra stood at the other end of the aisle, everything disappeared, and nothing else mattered. Everything we had been through, while tough, had brought us here. And as I looked at the woman I had once promised to love forever, I knew that I would make that promise again—and keep it.

In a blink, she was at my side, and I could barely hold back my grin. I didn't want to. I simply smiled at the woman in front of me and knew the others were whispering, all of them grinning. And when Arden began speaking, I leaned forward and brushed a single tear off Myra's cheek.

"I love you," I mouthed.

"I love you, too."

As the crowd cheered, and Arden pronounced us

husband and wife, I kissed the love of my life—my first, second, and last wife.

For more information please go to Carrie Ann's website
www.CarrieAnnRyan.com

A Note from Carrie Ann Ryan

Thank you so much for reading **FROM OUR FIRST.**

I loved this story. It was a little different for me but finding out how to keep these two together was a blast...even if they are so growly!

Next up from Carrie Ann is MY ONE NIGHT. Dillon and Elise are ready for their romance!

And in case you missed it, Arden and Liam might be familiar if you read Wrapped in Ink!

The Promise Me Series:

Book 1: Forever Only Once

Book 2: From That Moment

Book 3: Far From Destined

Book 4: From Our First

Want to read a special BONUS EPILOGUE featuring Nate & Myra? CLICK HERE!

About the Author

Carrie Ann Ryan is the New York Times and USA Today bestselling author of contemporary, paranormal, and young adult romance. Her works include the Montgomery Ink, Redwood Pack, Fractured Connections, and Elements of Five series, which have sold over 3.0 million books worldwide. She started writing while in graduate school for her advanced degree in chemistry and hasn't stopped since. Carrie Ann has written over seventy-five novels and novellas with more in the works. When she's not losing herself in her emotional and action-packed worlds, she's reading as much as she can while wrangling her clowder of cats who have more followers than she does.

www.CarrieAnnRyan.com

Made in the USA
Las Vegas, NV
13 December 2022

62221619R00177